Bok

MW00426249

PERSIANALITY

Young-Adult Thriller / Bildungsroman

Written by
Michael Benzehabe

Cover photo depicts
a scene in chapter 7, page 56
SHEMA PUBLISHING COMPANY
LOS ANGELES

PERSIANALITY

Copyright May 2019 by Michael Rankin/Agent

Requests for information should be addressed to:

Shema Publishing Company
Attn: Michael Rankin/Licensing Agent
516 N. Diamond Bar Blvd., #162
Diamond Bar, California 91765

Library of Congress Cataloging-in-Publication Data

Benzehabe, Michael,
Persianality / Michael Benzehabe

p. cm.
48,680 words, includes index.
ISBN-13: 9781095508442   /   ISBN-10: 109550844X
ASIN: B07QYMSXG7
1. YA Thriller. 2. YA Romance. 3. Bildungsroman.
Index Pending
File Pending
Cert Pending

(5.06 X 7.81) Acid-free paper. *48,680 words*.

Introduction

Who you become matters. And waste no time getting started. My first encounter with the *real* Jamileh Delkash—a skinny little thing—was when I witnessed her quarreling with an angry Muslim man.

As I looked up from my lunch I saw the man draw back and give her an awful slap. Rather than retreat, she launched into his face more ferocious than ever.

Don't ask me why, but I jumped over the patio's railing. By the time I reached this scoundrel, I had murder in my heart. I spun him around. I still remember the man's eyes blinking, anticipating my knuckles in his face.

That's when I felt the grip of her thin fingers on my arm. She was quick to assert her individualism and just as quick to protect the boundaries of others, even her enemies. She was quick to become a person who matters.

Many events described in this novel came from Jamileh's sisters. Jamileh refused to discuss these matters with me. So, I have no way to verify their authenticity, except by means of Noshahr's village gossip. There, I discovered Jamileh was more of a curiosity to her village than she was to me. And a complicated puzzle she was.

She lives on in the chimes of midnight, the epoch contained in every sigh. She had everything before her. A hybrid of Anne of Green Gables and Attila the Hun. The girl was crazy—a whirlwind of good intentions. God bless you Jamileh Delkash . . . wherever you are.

Michael Benzehabe

One

I dread dinner with Father. I dread his suffocating shroud of silence. I dread his end-of-day ritual. Most of all, I detest what comes last: his lock-up-for-the-night clatter. *Click, clang, grind, zing, clap, schlik*: horrid sounds. When those sounds first fell upon my ears, my blood ran cold. And so, by degrees, very gradually, I set my heart against Father.

You could synchronize your watch by this after-dinner ritual . . . and I don't wear his cage well. I shouldn't even be here. I belong with the one I love. I'm driven by the migration call of coupling, pulling me west, to nest in the sparkling lights of the Eiffel Tower.

Instead, I'm confined to this chair, listening to the metallic jangling of Father's steely knife against his silvery fork, dissecting his *Ras el hanout,* spiced leg of lamb. Dinner at the Delkash Compound. *Ugh!* Three teen daughters, Sarah, Zoe, and me, holding our tongues, hoping Father will speak, say something comforting, tell us our love will see us through. Anything to end the silence.

After dinner, we girls will be stacked away like fragile chinaware. Tomorrow, the cycle starts again. We'll be set out like decorative dinner plates, props for this craggy dining hall. Not exactly a Claude Monet cottage, more of a Medieval bastion—a vestige of Roman conquests. It still moans with the rickety sounds of age. I can almost hear the murmurs of ancient inhabitants.

How I long to run through our front gate, into the night. This new Iran has taken something from me, ripped a hole in my soul. Somewhere in this tumble, I worry if I've lost my moral certainty. Who knows what fell out, but a part of me is missing. That much is clear.

A teen can only conceal a crush for so long. Public flirtation is Iran's new crime and carries humiliating consequences. I'm in love . . . and almost fifteen.

Father has no idea what this has done to me. All that keeps me sane is knowing he is every bit the prisoner I am. He's empty, a slave to his medical practice, without hobbies, without friends, without a wife.

Mother is gone.

When one person is missing from the table, the whole world feels empty, hollow, echoing with voices of the past. All of us, from that time, have changed.

Love is so short.

Father no more knows how to console his daughters than we know how to console him. One could reason, he was more devastated by Mother's death than we were.

He's a pitiful soul. Gentle, frail, the least likely to protest. In a nation of hairy men, Father stands out like a sleek adolescent boy. For years, his hair was thin and wispy, then, in one year, gone. He couldn't even keep the hair on top of his head.

I suppose these things happen. Rage wears all of us down, eventually. At least it did with Father. He dawdles after dinner, intent on one thing: locking up for the night. A life in full retreat. He just can't muster the outrage or the fight to move on. Utterly without ambition.

I suspect other doctors make more than he does. Iran is the world's capital for nose jobs, but he's an endocrinologist. If we move to Tehran he could change his specialty and make a fortune. Gender reassignment surgeons are making a killing. In Tehran, it's not only legal, but partially funded by the government. Yet, the same legal system forbids homosexuality. One of many contradictions bundled in Iranian law.

Father, too, is a contradiction. The least heralded physician in Noshahr, a father too busy healing others to notice his daughters' broken hearts.

Not exactly true. I'm sure he notices. He just doesn't know what to do, and I don't know how to ask. So, here we are: him locking me in and me plotting my escape.

I haven't always felt this way. I once had an aesthetic eye for all things Iranian. I was raised on Mother's upbeat descriptions of Noshahr: a port city receptive to foreign ideas, Russian literature, Italian fashion, French perfumes. International intelligentsia was once openly envied—not quarantined. Mother was attracted to public squares where social lines were blurred, where different ideas and strange tongues taught solutions she could never imagine on her own.

From her upbeat descriptions, my expectations were so high that I almost missed our lapse into narrow-minded tyranny. Today's Noshahr has become a military sideshow, dangerous and malignant.

Nervous. Dreadfully nervous I've been. I know a fifteen-year-old woman (almost fifteen) shouldn't say such things, but I'm starting to discover a lot of new womanly hazards that Mother never discussed. We girls face risky propositions. Probably because Father doesn't frighten the village blackguards. They probably sense he came undone after Mother's death, when we needed him most.

A lot of new things are starting to occur to me. Supposedly, the only route to Allah is through your father. But anyone who thinks their father is the final authority is an idolater. Again, I shouldn't say such things, but as I sit here, at the dinner table, a lot of new thoughts are telling me new and exciting truths.

As I look around our dining room, its walls groan with a great waste of years. Even the hinges squeak to me in rusty laments. So pointless to play over how our years might have been put to better use. They can't be recovered now. We do well not to grieve on and on. Ancient voices may have much to tell, but no one's listening.

Iran . . . this strange and depressing place. This Ayatollah wasteland is where I gather with friends and watch their eyes scream *Let me out!*

I will find peace.

I will hear angels.

I will see a sky that sparkles with diamonds.

Until then, I sit here with a mouth full of halva, realizing that there is no situation so bad that I can't make it worse. I've done it. I lied to Father . . . to spare him. I broke our family rule: better to hurt with the truth than comfort with a lie.

I woke up today with a list of his expectations and I'm tiring of it. Tomorrow, I'm heading for the Monkey Bar to clear my thoughts of Father's antiquated prohibitions.

Why aren't parents making peace with the new truths? And I have a lot of truth that could cause a lot of hurt.

Two

This is reckless.

Away from prying eyes, I creep down the back alley of the notorious Monkey Bar. My target? A tin-clad service door, surrounded by garbage bins, dented and disorderly. I only want a peek, one small glimpse of *him*.

This dreadful fringe of ill-estate does its best to drive me away with its smelly barrier of GO AWAY! It reeks of restaurant scrapings.

Reckless.

But, here I am, at *his* favorite spot. I stretch forward, ear first, and hear raucous gamblers inside, placing bets, calling apron-wearing chimps to their tables, ordering American Coca-Colas. I hear the grunts of trained monkeys, waiting tables. I can picture them opening sodas with jewel-encrusted bottle openers. A gimmick, to be sure, but all Noshahr loves the novelty. Quite the success, generating stacks and stacks of wooden crates, filled with empty Coke bottles. The empties line the stone wall behind me.

Undeterred by the malodor of commerce, I gather my chador to cover my nose as I inch closer. My Italian Valentinos step lightly over cobblestones, still slick with garbage more stubborn than hose and broom. I force myself to touch the door's filthy handle, but freeze in place after hearing a rustle behind me. In a breathless panic, I spin about. My vision narrows to a spot half-way up the wooden crates. Squinting, I force my eyes to acclimate to its shaded recesses.

Deep in the shadows, a hot ember from a lit cigarette glows. For a brief second, the light illumes the face of the famous chimp, Bosco, champion bicyclist. He stares back, emotionless, unimpressed. His relentless gaze makes me uncomfortable, self-conscious, intimidated.

"I'm not here to steal anything," I say, bright and cheery. "I just wanted to take a quick look inside." I tilt my head toward the door, hint-hint style.

Bosco says nothing.

"How did you get out of your cage?" I ask.

Bosco's lips fall into a crooked sneer. *Face Mail.* He didn't like that question.

"I won't tell anyone. I just want to know if a special someone is inside. So, if you don't mind . . ."

Bosco relaxes, still holding his cigarette between two nicotine-stained fingers.

"You shouldn't smoke, you know. If you were serious about bicycle racing, you would know smoking diminishes your lung capacity."

Bosco's hand stabs forward, flicking his mostly-finished cigarette. It twirls through the air like a Molotov cocktail, barely missing me, but after striking the tin-clad door, sparks explode in all directions.

Badditude!

My hands fly everywhere at once. After a quick going-over, I surmise nothing is aflame. Silk and sparks, a hazardous combination. "You're a very bad monkey!" I say, lashing my finger, inches from Bosco's face. "I was only expressing civil concern about your wellbeing. That's no way to respond to well-intended discourse."

He ignores me and flips a fresh cigarette high in the air, catching it between his lips, like some sort of a movie star. He cuts his eyes at me, defiantly, raising a Bic to kindle his fresh smoke.

What an insolent monkey.

"Well, I-I'm just g-going to look inside," I whisper.

Bosco stares into the distance, like I am no longer worthy of his attention. He had always seemed so well behaved on the race track—like a real gentleman. I must confess, I thought he was better than this. But, I presume his non-response to be consent. So, I place one hand on the door, watching Bosco's reaction. Warily, I turn the doorknob and pull.

The worst place to be in Iran is a dank alley, standing in front of a service entrance, in Italian heels. I don't know what damp icky thing I'm standing on, but it's better than going inside. Inside, testosterone-driven young men gamble on monkey races.

Love is such a thoughtless master. It gives no consideration to the dignity of its victim. Lately, I'd often stopped at places beneath my station—for love. At this stage, I doubt myself, regret the depth I've sunk . . . just to be seen . . . by *him*.

Reckless.

I'm overdressed for the Monkey Bar, but this is where fellow teens gather, *Armand* in particular.

Why young men enjoy gambling is beyond me. But, who am I? A helpless dupe of love. That's who.

He has no idea how carefully I preserve his sparse greetings, fractured sentences, distracted farewells. With tweezers-of-hope and a microscope-of-desperation, I always rush home, anxious to examine and re-examine his every word, hoping to discover a beginning—some flicker of interest.

Any word from *him* gives me just enough sustenance, because I always come back, hungering for more. I treasure every word, dissect how they were delivered, *re*-live them, *re*-taste them, *re*-breathe them, longing to find a trace of reciprocal love. If only he would give me a sign. I would do my part.

How can I nudge a boy's level of interest forward? What I need is some pretense to start a meaningful conversation. I could start with something jolly. Conversations are always lighthearted when discussing one's own shortcomings. Nothing too close to truth, of course. Maybe some confession of daring. Nothing comes to mind, but with a little thought I could invent something frivolous, or even cute.

No, too risky. May Allah forgive my sordid visits to the Monkey Bar, but I have it bad for Armand.

Reckless.

Without warning, a violent force slams the door, and very nearly amputates my nose! I jump back, every nerve ringing like an automatic fire alarm. Staring down at me is six-foot of ill-tempered authority. Basij.

Anticipointment!

They are such dictators. The slammed door is their signature authoritarian move, a power punctuation mark. The Moral Police are all about exaggerated energy, balled fists, barked orders, just to see us flinch.

Moral Police are a new phenomenon, since the demise of the Shah. He wears the traditional light-brown, nearly-non-descript uniform. On his head, a tied Shemagh scarf. The big policeman steps back to eye me up. In his right hand, he sports a leather riding crop, smacking the other hand with the lash end to create an intimidating *pop*, a sound that could just as well be on my backside.

Normally, the Basij patrol busy shopping stalls, anxious to find violators of Islamic propriety, but given his aggressive posture, I fear I might be today's victim. I cringe like a mouse at a cat party, not half as courageous as I imagined I would be. "Sir . . . I want to go home."

Dark and foreboding, he glares at me with a face full of rules.

"I was peeking inside to find my driver. I had an intuition that he might be—"

"I know the good doctor's driver," he interrupts.

By *good doctor* he implied that he knew my father, Dr. Delkash, Iran's worst endocrinologist. Whether his reference was sarcasm, I couldn't tell.

"Your driver sent me. But I never expected to find you at the backdoor of a gambling house."

Apparently, he has no intention of beating me. I draw a shaky breath and exhale slowly, preparing to squeak out an alibi of some type. "Food establishment. The Monkey Bar."

He responds with a smug grunt. "There are many things you don't know. What are you, fourteen?"

"Sixteen!" I say, firm and sassy. I wasn't sixteen. But his tone made fourteen sound so vapid, made me sound unworthy of intelligent thought.

For the first time, he notices Bosco, luxuriating on the discarded Coca-Cola boxes. The policeman's body language changes, squaring off against the uncaged monkey.

"Run along," he says, without looking back. "Your driver is out front."

Muscles relax, to the point that I slouch. A big sigh, almost a sob, leaks out. Never one to waste an escape, I march quickly toward the end of the alley, longing for the protection of my dear Uncle Solomon. Before turning the corner, I glance back. The officer's hands are firmly planted on his hips, staring at the smoking chimp. The monkey sits back, unperturbed, fearless, taking a long drag off his cigarette, staring straight back.

A power stare down, I suppose.

What a brave monkey . . . but, reckless.

Three

Begging Giti appears from nowhere and blocks my escape from the Basij. Her hair is properly covered, but her bangs are dusty and unbrushed. I see fresh bug bites, which says a lot about the cleanliness of the orphanage. We've been friends, on and off, for years, but she's mostly friendless, the wrong type, always subverting a simple greeting into a handout.

How can a simple description do her justice? Despite some of the aforementioned details, she is attractive, well-formed, even graceful.

Her first impression never makes literal sense, if you pull on any one thread, but as an entire garment, she fascinates me. Seven plot twists in this girl's bio . . . and she's only sixteen.

"Jamileh!" she pleads, both hands extended. "Alms for a meal? When I got back from prayer service the kitchen had closed."

"Allah will provide," I say, finger toward heaven. I try pushing past her. I don't like it when Giti gets handsy with my purse. She said *alms* as if my money's sole purpose is to solve her problems. I'm as generous— *more* generous than most. I just don't like poor people. They contribute very little to the national economy.

I continue with my classic above-it-all peel away. "Please!" I say, pushing her hands away. "Uncle Solomon is watching."

Uncle Solomon leans against Father's car, no more than forty feet away. He signals me by pointing to his wrist watch—just a Timex.

"That's your uncle? My! He looks like a man of means, with that uniform and fancy motor car. Is he a doctor, too?"

"I meant *Uncle* as a term of endearment. Mother found him, washed up on the lip of the Caspian Sea. Just a child of eleven, long before we took in Zoe."

"An orphan?"

"He's too old to be an orphan, now. Twenty, before you ask." I didn't dare tell her that he's training on bicycles for the Olympics, and has muscles—butt muscles. If she found that out, she'd be all over him.

"A grown man," she purrs, "with a sad story, no doubt."

"A tragic story. My mother shared a few details. He and his sisters were kidnapped by Afghan slavers. Of course they had no need for a boy. They threw him overboard. Allah must have been with him, because Father gave him quarters over the carriage house in exchange for a few menial tasks. We grew to love him . . . over the years."

"So he became your driver?"

"Eventually. That's a driver's uniform, not a doctor's. At fifteen, his duties expanded to include driving Father to and from the hospital." I didn't like the way Giti stared at Uncle Solomon. Maybe I was more afraid Uncle Solomon would return her interest. I—all of us—hope he'll find a good marriage. Giti would not be a good marriage. No dowry.

"Anyway," Giti says, "he certainly gets more than his share of attention with that big fancy Rolls Royce. Is he a good Muslim?"

Beware if a Muslim girl asks how observant a man is. She has designs. There is no better way to nail a man's feet to the floor than fastening him with verses from the Koran. "Spotty, at best," I answer. "He loves that Rolls more than Father does. But, all in all, Uncle Solomon is okay."

Giti was right about one thing: Uncle Solomon's uniform and Father's car were painfully out of place in our small village. But that's Noshahr, full of contradictions: smugglers flush with cash rubbed shoulders with powerful under lords as they strolled side-by-side in the same tiny fishing village. Tehran's politicians built expensive vacation homes along Noshahr's beautiful northern coast. Their modern homes glitter along the shoreline with electric lights, while more traditional homes, such as ours, are still lit with oil lamps.

As Iran's northernmost port, Noshahr serves as the unofficial backdoor. The docks are populated with a wild mix of races, coming and going at all hours of the night. Russians, North Koreans, are forever shuttling contraband beneath the noses of our indifferent port authorities. Wayward youth buy strange things off foreign boats without maritime registration numbers. Unlike the rest of Iran, Noshahr is more like a foreign city, riding all manner of cultural margins.

Servicing this nest of vipers was how Father came to possess such a car. It arrived one moonless night as payment for the medical services he performed on

Osama Bin Laden. It seems Osama is diabetic, like Mother . . . the succumbed.

Father isn't the sort of man who notices fancy cars, but when a warlord offered one, in lieu of cash, he took it. Quibbling over such a matter could be interpreted as ingratitude, which brings ugly consequences. *It's better than a donkey*, Father often says.

I notice that Uncle Solomon and Giti are sharing a peculiar smile. She has an alarming sparkle in her eyes that worries me. I dare not let that kindle.

He motions for us to come closer.

"You'd better go," I say. "He has to rush me home. Father finishes his rounds in a few hours. Can't be late."

Giti frowns and stomps one foot. "Oh Jamileh, are you sure you don't have something jingling around in one of those fancy pockets?"

"No! Meet me here tomorrow. Lunch will be on me. I'll introduce you to my new friend. She's wealthy, you know, someone who may hire you for respectable work."

Giti grips my arm as she draws a joyful breath. As annoying as she is, she has a sweet side. I blush at such a demonstration. After she gives a quick kiss to my forehead she scampers off.

Show time.

With Giti out of the way, I ease into the new me— Lolita-Jamileh. My walk slows, letting my spine find the rhythm between my hips and shoulders. Belly dancing has provided me with a treasure-trove of feminine wiles. Gait bait. When I want to, my hips roll, undulate . . . but not in a tawdry way.

I lower my chin and peer over the rims of my Moscot sunglasses.

In perfect chauffeur protocol, Uncle Solomon opens the curbside passenger door and stands at attention.

"Thank you for holding my door, Uncle Solomon." I too have been trained in proper manners. Always thank someone with a full sentence.

I slide inside the *Monstrosity*, as my sisters call it, grip the seatbelt, stare at it. But I'm unable, unwilling, afraid to buckle it. It's back. Confinement. I feel an icy paralysis rising from the pit of my stomach, curling past my throat, leaving me bug-eyed and in a panic.

Uncle Solomon starts the car while I sit frozen, unable to fasten this automotive straightjacket.

"Seatbelts," he reminds.

"You have a bumper," I snap. "Use it." I just hate it when I behave that way. If only I could rid myself of this incarceration phobia.

Uncle Solomon wags a scolding finger. "You know the Doctor's five rules for car travel."

I kick the back of his seat and plead, "Could you help me with this? I can't seem—"

In a flash, he has my door open, reaching for my buckle. I slap his hand away. I can't help it. I need his help, but can't stand being buckled in. He reaches again. I don't want to, but I push his hand away.

"What is wrong, Jamileh?"

"I don't know," I confess, close to tears. "I can't stand the thought of restraint. It feels like . . . slow death."

"That is okay. You can buckle yourself."

"No. You do it. It gives me visions of *Jahannam*. I feel trapped, like I'm in girl jail."

"Girl jail?"

"You know what I'm talking about—imprisoned by cultural restraints, secreted away from life—real life."

Uncle Solomon gives his usual sigh of helpless irritation. "Oh, that again." He snatches the buckle from my hand, nearly breaking a nail, and attaches my seatbelt with an authoritative *click*. "Hang on little sister, we will be home in a few minutes."

"Thank you," I say, fanning myself.

As we speed away, he adjusts his rear-view mirror until our eyes meet. He gives me a sympathetic wink. "You told me you were going across the street, not the Monkey Bar."

Perspiration beads across my forehead, not because he caught me in a lie, but because of girl jail. I'm glad to hear the air conditioner crank up. I let my head fall back against the cool leather seat. The outside heat had been stifling, but the car's refrigerated air begins to revive me. "School is wrong about everything."

I catch his cynical smile in the mirror.

I don't mind his skepticism, because I have earth-shattering news. "Freud was a fool," I announce. "Can you imagine it? Love, a byproduct of base human drives? What an emotionally constipated fool. And Young! He claimed love is a chemical reaction to circumstance, stress, reproduction, and the primal need for shelter. What I know is better than a Ph.D. In the real world, people fall in love, and it's beautiful."

The car comes to a sudden dirt-grinding halt. The dust rolls past my window. As it clears, I see Uncle Solomon opening my door. With his driver's cap, he fans me—as if I need fanning.

"Think, little Jamileh. You will outgrow this." He turns my chin to face him. "In a few years you will find the proper mindset. Then, you will commute like royalty, preordained for the back of a limo." He shrugs. "Panic attack. That is all."

My words are not the result of a panic attack. I try to conceal my ecstasy, but words burst from my voice box, setting off a chat geyser. "I'm not a little girl anymore. Go ahead, mark your calendar. Today, I'm a woman. Suddenly, I'm alert to all things uniting the hearts of God's good creatures. I know what turns the hearts of birds at Spring time. I feel what every wild deer feels. I have the feeling of forever in my heart."

"Forever?"

"Yes. One afternoon last week, I woke up, and I was suddenly alive, conscious, bright as a star. I love emotion. I love being in love. There's no changing your mind when that sort of thing happens, because there's no mind to change. It's a glorious persianality disorder."

"Persianality?"

"Yes. There's a world out there, a world made for love. Love is—"

My phobia wouldn't even permit me to finish my sentence. Panic rises from deep within. Kicking and swinging my arms, I try to rip free from the grip of my seatbelt. Somewhere in this red blur of hysteria, Uncle Solomon fishes me out and seats me on the back fender.

A few minutes of recuperation pass. I gaze up at a sky tipping toward the pinkish-yellow side of the color scale. Despite the heat, the fresh air rolling off the Caspian works its magic, soothing me, calming me. I stand and pace, arms folded, my mind still spinning with fizzy thoughts of Armand.

Uncle Solomon remains seated on the back bumper's chrome lip, content to watch me pace. "You never have these fits on the way to market, only on the way home."

"It's just exhaustion," I say.

Eyes as warm as fresh bread, Uncle Solomon sighs. "I have considered that possibility. Or, maybe it is the destination. Lately, you do not seem happy at home."

Too close to truth! A subject I had no intention of discussing with him. I continue to pace, back and forth. I turn toward the Caspian. A soft sea breeze cools my face. "Noshahr can be a deceptively beautiful place. I mean, it's not exactly Paris. 'Gay Paree!' they call it, where love is celebrated.

"Not to demean Paris," says Uncle Solomon, "but Iran has plenty to celebrate—regarding love, I mean."

It's all I can do to hide my contempt. "May Allah forgive me, but look what the Revolutionary Guard has done to my town. Noshahr has become a pressure cooker of unhappy women, generation on generation, with no forks in the road, no surprise around the corner. Maybe you don't feel it the way I do, because I lead a one-dimensional life, with only one destination. Marriage."

"Is that why you husband-shop at the Monkey Bar?"

The nerve! I stretch forward and strike his shoulder. "Stop that. Why do you make me sound so desperate?"

Uncle Solomon shrugs, but doesn't take it back.

"Sadly, even marriage would improve this empty life of mine," I confess. "But, it's the ever-after that frightens me. Walk down any street. You'll see all those 'ever-after' wives. Have you counted the missing smiles?"

Uncle Solomon's fingers drum across his knee. "Take heart. When people get older they discover unexpected treasures in hometowns. Eventually, their place of origin has a transcendent pull that no adventure, no romance, no handsomely furnished vacation home can ever match. Atavistic."

I resume my pacing. It helps me think. "Preaching," I accuse.

"Preaching?" he responds quizzically. "No. My point is quite secular, homespun even. Noshahr has its share of happy families."

"Maybe, but my future is in Paris."

"Paris?"

"Isn't it obvious? Armand said I was made for Paris."

"Armand? The son of our Ambassador to France?"

"Yes. If anyone would know, he would." I knew after the words left my mouth that Uncle Solomon didn't take me seriously. Every time I mentioned Armand, that's when the conversation stopped. "Promise me one thing." I stoop until we're eye-to-eye. "Never tell Father."

He got it. I could tell by his reluctant nod.

"But France?" he grumbles. "They love frogs, snails . . . Proust! Do not let those sons-of-politicians shape your thoughts. Dismiss such talk and tattle. You are better than all of them. And it pains me that you do not see it."

Was that a compliment? The sudden glow from my feverish cheeks embarrasses me. I turn away to hide the pleasure it gives me. What a day. First Giti made me blush, now Uncle Solomon. "Thank you," I say. "But never tell Father how unhappy I am. The truth would probably kill him."

Uncle Solomon stands then bows, his new annoying gesture of submission. The one designed to remind me that he wasn't part of our biological family. "He is a better man than you know, but I will leave you two to work that out. I, however, would be less than honest if I did not confess how much your despair pains me."

In this unguarded instant, I realize how much I miss my childhood-big-brother, Uncle Solomon. I miss the comfortable merriment we once shared. His face is awash with a transitioning auburn from the setting sun. It is a handsome face, maybe the only pleasing face left in this wretched town . . . besides Armand's.

"I think it was your melancholy that inspired the poem I wrote last night." His voice softens into lulling cadences—unexpectedly enticing.

Everyone in Iran fancies themselves poets. But Uncle Solomon? Of all men, I never would have guessed that he wrote poetry. Then again, I didn't know he read Proust. That surprised me, too. "A pretty poem?"

"Not a pretty poem, more of a presentiment."

Not that I didn't trust him, but poetry seems too far-fetched. "Recite it."

Uncle Solomon clears his throat:

"The yearning wave
Slams the barrier wall
Fighting for its liberty
When the wall succumbs
The wave falls through
Onto the desert floor
Free
But perishes
Beneath freedom's baking sun."

Four

"Be still!" Mornings were the only hours I had Zoe to myself. I grabbed both her shoulders and gave them a shake. Then, I lifted her chin and lipsticked French curves on her upper lip.

"This better not be Sarah's makeup," Zoe complained.

"It's Mother's. She left it to me."

"Oh."

Truth? I bought it with my own money in Azadi Square, but Zoe never challenged me on matters pertaining to Mother. *Never intrude on someone's grief.* "Of course we were still alive after Mother died, but as a family, we've been gradually dying, ever since. Grief is the final act of love," I sighed.

We all knew nostalgia was dangerous. I hastily wiped a tear away, then turned quickly until we were nose to nose. "Here's a tip: When you see grief in the eyes of a stranger, or me, you're seeing uprooted love, gasping its last breath. Be kind to these poor souls. All the pretty pictures that sparked holiday memories have passed . . . and memories are all we have."

Zoe smiled sympathetically, but as a thirteen year old, I didn't think she understood the full impact of my sufferings. Yet, it was easy to forgive her. Maybe because few things gave me greater satisfaction than dressing her up. She was my human doll (Sarah's too).

Father brought her home a few weeks back. Sarah and I have often fought over her. This morning, she

was mine. I sat her at my vanity while I brushed
highlights across her cheek bones for that gaunt look
that's so popular in Hollywood.

I had been in homes with electricity and automatic
televisions. Show Biz was my life—to the extent it
could be.

I liked the gaunt look on Zoe. So, I dabbed
Dermabond along her upper cheekbones and applied
glitter. *Magnifique!* I didn't realize I had it in me, but
with my help Zoe bore a striking resemblance to
Anicee Alvina, Iran's most glamorous actress. *Ooh la
la!* I must commit this process to memory. Who
knows, maybe Armand sees a little Anicee in me.

Zoe's eyes narrowed to an accusatory glare. She
could always tell when I thought about boys. She and
Sarah had teamed up to become a joy-killing duo.
They never liked it when I discussed boys. Father had
yet to choose our potential husbands. Sarah believed
boy-thoughts should be repressed until a designated
husband provided a proper face for such thoughts.

So tribal.

"What I'm about to say will sound terrible, or, I
should say, it will make me sound terrible—but I'm
not!

"I hate my father.

"Not HATE hate, but disappointment hate.
Mother died from diabetes, and he's an
endocrinologist. Apparently, not a very good one—
despite his never-ending five-step remedies. Naturally,

he had a five-step remedy for her diabetes. Step One, exercise; Step Two, diet; Step Three, weight (he kept Mother at a trim one-hundred pounds); Step Four, vitamins (C, D, E, B6, and niacin bound GTF chromium. He was big on digestive enzymes, too); Step Five, attitude. And *no* hookah pipes. She ignored the hookah pipe injunction, when her friends stayed over.

"You may not know this, Zoe, but we loved your father, Dr. Mousa. I'll always be thankful that he interned for my father. Your father begged to have Mother transferred to a modern Israeli hospital, but Father was convinced Iran's medical facilities were the best in the world . . . along with his five-step remedy.

Eventually, when it was too late, Father realized Israel *had* developed worthwhile procedures and set about filing transfer documents. This pushed us into some sort of Kafkaesque bureaucratic nightmare of endless appointments, never resulting in passports.

"Do you know who Kafka is?"

Zoe nodded, but I had my doubts.

"Do you know who Anne of Green Gables is?" she asked.

"No. Why?"

"You talk a lot."

"I have lots of thoughts. I've never stopped you from talking. If you have something to say, say it."

"No," she said. "I like it when you talk." She turned her cheek to me, expecting more glitter.

"Well, anyway, I just have one more thing to say. Maybe I'm the Himalayas of audacity; a desert whirlwind of circular logic; a raging rapids of rashness, but Mother relied on him, and so did I. Maybe I'm creating an inverted Shakespearean play where I relive Mother's missed opportunities instead of living in my present reality. I don't know.

"He can be caustically positive about all things Persian. Yet, to his credit, he never tried to put a positive spin on his medical abilities. Even he knew he failed Mother. He failed all of us, actually. I ignore Father. You've probably noticed.

"Is 'ignore' the proper word? I do know I'm silently waiting for something. A confession? Tears? An apology? Who knows? Truth be told, I'm not sure he's capable. He's not exactly in the present either. As the supreme leader of our family, losing her must have hit him hardest. He works more, smokes hashish more, and compulsively applies five-step solutions to everything. He's become what the French call *obsede*.

"I don't know if you've noticed, but I speak a lot of French, lately." I waited for her acknowledgement, maybe even a tribute.

Nothing.

"So when I say 'everything,' I mean *everything*: getting in a car, getting out of a car, doing homework, and the one that sends me up a wall . . . locking up for the night."

Earlier, Zoe flinched at the word *hashish*. That made me suspicious. I brought her close, face to face.

"These are family matters—private matters. Our family problems must never be repeated outside this house. Understand?"

Zoe nodded in bobble-headed yes's. She's not the gossiping sort. I believed her.

"We already had a twenty-foot wall around the entire compound, but stirred by his new paranoias Father brought in blacksmiths from Tehran. They bolted spikes—razor-sharp spikes—atop the outer walls, and installed thick iron latches on our entry gate. Within the walls, our house was refitted with iron bolts for every door, iron bars over every window. The noise the installers made. Ugh! I nearly died from all their hammering and filing. I have a condition, a medical condition. Claustrophobia."

Zoe gave me a gimlet-eyed stare, roundly unconvinced.

I smacked her on the shoulder. "Really!"

I took a deep breath. I could no longer deny it. We had a new embarrassment in the Delkash household: Zoe's Jewishness. Our new Doubting Thomas still had some rough edges.

Father brought her into our home a few weeks back, after her parents were murdered. From a Jewish household to a Muslim household. No orientation. No counseling. No re-education. I heard Sarah whisper to Father about a crash course at Commisceo Global. They have cultural training courses. I watched him nodding and rubbing his chin, as though he was giving it serious thought.

Nothing came of it.

MICHAEL BENZEHABE   28   PERSIANALITY

Father didn't even change her religion. Quite the opposite. He charged me to let her worship as she pleased. So, she lacks, as the French say, *graces sociales*. That could make her interactions with Iran's upper class embarrassing. Not that she isn't smart, she just lacks the background, the foundation, or good Persian genetics.

The moment seemed right. It was high time to overcome her genetic deficit. It was my calling, my mission, my God-given duty to acclimate her to the life of a Delkash—good and bad.

No better place to start than wardrobe. "Zoe, I'm about to prepare you for a very special transition." I opened my dresser and removed a carved wooden box that held the jewels Mother left me. It wasn't much: a large diamond ring and a string of iridescent pearls.

"*Hmm*," I mused. What she needed was royal radiance. "Wait here. Sarah has better stuff in her room, a virtual museum of the extraordinary."

"No," Zoe protested, wide-eyed. "I don't want Sarah mad at me."

I covered my mouth, giggling. "Are you kidding? We're Persians living in the same household, eating the same food, drinking the same water. Sharing jewelry is a bond of solidarity, not robbery." I knew this was a lie, but over time, I intended to correct all the moral details. Not tonight, but over time.

I returned from Sarah's room with a tiara, bracelets, and extravagant ruby earrings.

Item by item, I adorned our little Jew with Persia's best. I circled her, smiling, laughing. She looked deliciously preposterous. Over dressed, a fake princess in a poorly plumbed compound, without electricity. She loved it. While she paraded with exaggerated shakes and wiggles, I applauded and shouted all the things that bad boys say to pretty girls. Posing, belly dancing, catwalking, soon we were too tired to stand.

As we lay on my bed, I suddenly realized how best to bring her up to *princess* speed. First of all, she needed to feel the history we lived in. She already knew every inch of architecture, but what she really needed was a cultural *ghusl*.

"I have a painful confession: The Delkash compound is a charade. A fraud. Our neighbors think we're rich because we live inside huge walls of stone with two imposing towers."

None of this lit a flame of recognition in Zoe's eyes.

I walked to my bedroom door and swung it open. "Come." Zoe hurried close behind. I intended to start my own version of a Commisceo Seminar on our upstairs terrace. I led her outside and leaned over the terrace's railing. I closed my eyes to inhale the scent of jasmine, rising from below."

"Careful," she said, gripping the back of my hijab.

I turned and removed her grabby little hand. "Relax, little sister. A rooftop parapet can be a magical place after midnight. Uncle Solomon lives up there, in the third story of the north tower, and our cook, Auntie Esther, lives over there in the south tower. From their rooms, they oversee the outer walls. We rely on their sharp eyes to spot unseemly characters lurking outside.

That was the duty of tower guards in ancient Persia.
Uncle Solomon's third-story room allows him to see
the girls' otherwise private second-story terrace." I
shrugged. "Every safety has a privacy tradeoff.

"You've probably noticed our compound is set
atop an elevated mound, but what passers-by don't see
is that, over the ages, soil has buried the first story.
Originally, this was a three-story fortress with four-
story towers."

Zoe's eyebrows arched. I knew what she was
thinking: a secret basement she'd never explored. A
whole new secret world!

"Don't get your hopes up, little sister. Bulgarian
craftsmen talked Father into burying our first floor.
They said digging away the sediment would only
create a funnel. Prone to flood at the next hard rain.
Better to fill the hole, add a few more feet to create a
grade that repels water. You know . . . better drainage.
It would have been less expensive to build a whole
new house somewhere else, the South of France, for
instance.

"And by the way, Bulgarians shake their head
when they mean yes, and nod when they mean no.

"Father, being no craftsman, and confused by
their nodding and shaking, decided to let the
Bulgarians do whatever they wanted. There went our
former first floor. Buried. That left us with a twenty-
foot surround, a two-storied residence, three-storied
towers, and a rooftop terrace with balustrades. Father
said that was more than enough."

Zoe slouched, disappointed. She soon raised her head, however, this time with a pensive glare. "Then the outer walls must have been thirty feet, at one time."

I glared back, resenting her interruption. "Well, the Bulgarians only mentioned the house. But, now that you mention it, that probably included the outer walls."

I took Zoe's ring hand and balled it into a fist. "This might be a very expensive diamond. Don't let it slip off your finger. It's my inheritance." I said this while shaking a dangerous finger in her face. I meant it as a no-joke threat.

"Anyway, our compound must have been something to behold in its glory days, around 1700, before gas, electric, indoor plumbing, and air conditioning. At least we have copper plumbing, thanks to the Bulgarians.

"The previous owner told Father it was built in the Safavid Dynasty and survived an attack by Nader Shah. He showed us burn marks and melted lead on some of the foundation stones. Maybe this was true, and maybe it wasn't. I say that, because the previous owner lied about so many other features.

"He also said, 'The old place had been pumiced by heroic lives of departed generations.' And that too was probably a lie. It sounded pretty at the time, but I have no idea what it means.

"But, Mother's eyes lit up when she repeated the *supposed* history to guests. Everything sounded better when she told it. She made our compound sound special, more enchanted than modern homes along the coast that sparkled with modern electricity."

Zoe's chin rose. "I think it's better."

"Carefrontation! Not really. I know you're new here, but if you think about it, we don't have automatic lights. That's what I meant by *charade*."

Five

It was clear Zoe had stars in her eyes, a little too enthusiastic about her new home—our home. I wasn't sure what manner of house she came from, but I was starting to hold her opinion suspect. I continued. "After burying the old first floor, Father brought in more craftsmen, mostly Afghan migrants. They converted the north tower's new bottom level into a carriage house, where Uncle Solomon parks the *Monstrosity*. They added a big bowed iron door that matched the arc of the tower wall. It slides on overhead tracks. It's so well balanced that even a girl like me could slide it open with one hand."

Zoe nodded, as though my words resolved a question she was about to ask. Maybe she planned on stealing our car and racing off to Israel. Based on her father's stellar reputation I dismissed the thought, but we barely knew her—that much was certain.

She took my hand as if to test my garage-door skills. She bent my hand at the wrist, spread my fingers, then bent each finger at its joint. Without so much as a smile, she nodded her approval.

She's a serious little thing. Apparently, I had passed her garage-door opening test . . . as if I needed her approval.

I jerked my hand back. "I'm telling you this in bare-minimalistic-skeletal outline." I moved my hand to my hidden side. With a stolen glance, I checked for whatever mysterious indicators Zoe had searched for, but it was the same old hand. What's with that girl?

"At one time our huge car appeared small, with all the extra space in the carriage house. Then, Uncle Solomon started storing his personal effects: exercise equipment, bicycles, barrels, and tools. Now, parking is a tight fit. Ever wonder why Uncle Solomon drops us off at the front gate? We can't open the passenger doors after he pulls inside. How would he like it if we stored our things in his room, upstairs?

"When I brought this to Father's attention he mumbled something about wishing he had something to put in the garage. Until then, Uncle Solomon was free to store any items he wanted, since, as our driver, it was his space to manage as he saw fit.

"Father is so oblivious. He too is a twenty-foot wall, inaccessible, immovable, walling me away from everything. He's the real wall that blocks me; the real boundary of my universe. If only I could see his other side. Laughter bounces off walls. Humor bounces off Father. Hard to imagine myself in that outside world, but lately, I've stepped over some of his boundaries and I like the way it feels."

Quick to Father's defense, Zoe leaned in assertively. "Dr. Delkash seems nice to me."

I cautioned her with a wink. "'Seems' is the operative word." Moving on, I extended my arm, making a horizontal sweep of our terrace. "Up here is where he makes me grow our decorative flowers: lilies of the Nile, birds of paradise, tulips, roses."

"Let me tend the garden," Zoe said. "I'll take care of it."

"No! I didn't say it wasn't enjoyable. I just wanted to demonstrate how demanding he can be.

"You can't see the flowers from below because I position them behind the parapets. I separate each batch with terracotta vases filled with miniature lime trees." I almost swooned at the thought of lime zest on stewed lamb. "The lime trees smell like heaven.

"I let the bougainvilleas drip over the wall, with their majestic scarlet blossoms. They grow fast in this heat. Uncle Solomon has to cut them back every three months or so.

"I didn't mean to cut you off earlier, but the roof garden is mine. It's the only living thing that keeps me connected to Mother. It used to be hers.

"But, you can help keep an eye out for destructive seasonal winds. Ancient Afghan caravans named our worst wind 'The Wind That Kills Goats.' Such winds could scorch Mother's delicate garden. I tend these flowers with the same care I gave Mother when I fetched her water, in those sad and final months.

"You can pick a few flowers for your room. I don't mind, as long as you don't get crazy with it."

I brought Zoe to the right side of our terrace and leaned over the railing, pointing. "Below, to the right of Uncle Solomon's tower, is the only gate into the compound. You know, where he drops us off. That gate has large planks of cedar from Lebanon and huge iron hinges from Rome. Indestructible. It's always locked, which means visitors wait outside, until I unlock it. Or, Father could leave it unlocked. Of course, that will never happen. Thank goodness the compound's walls are thick. That means visitors can wait within the gate's shaded keystoned arch, until I open it. See it?

"Since I hate locks, could you unlock the front gate—make it your duty?"

Zoe, anxious to please, agreed immediately, but soon her face clouded as she reconsidered the gate below. "What would I have to do?"

"Nothing much," I assured her. "As of late, we never have guests and Father arrives at the same time every evening, about six. Wait for his knock; open the face plate, just to be sure it's him, then, and only then, unbolt the gate. Never unlock the gate for anyone other than Father. That's the rule."

Her smile returned. "That's easy."

"Easy if you don't have claustrophobia." I zeroed in for signs of skepticism. Earlier she doubted my delicate condition. This time, not so much as a batted lash. Apparently, she had come to terms with it.

No need to hit her.

A cool breeze from the Caspian blew through our hijabs, poofing our garments out like sails on two small ships. I placed a hand on each thigh to keep my clothing from blowing over my head. The wind swirled deliciously around my bare skin and its fluttering fingers clambered beneath my headscarf. How lovely to stand two stories up, as if gliding on every breeze, like a bird hovering above our beautiful courtyard.

When the wind died, I pointed below. "Inside the entry, laborers tiled the courtyard with Moroccan tile. Father got a discount, because the Moroccans already had them in production for a famous restaurant in California. That's in the United States. Did you know that?"

Zoe nodded.

For a thirteen year old, she claimed to know an awful lot. Seemed a little unlikely, as I thought about it. "Ferns and other shade-loving plants grow alongside the inner walls. On the far-left side we used to have a fountain with a statue, Anahita, the Persian goddess of water. Father tore it out and built a wading pool for Mother, but she filled it with fish and made it a lily pond. Sarah hogs that space. You know, elder sister privilege. You've probably seen her lounge beside it for hours, usually with a book, but she hardly ever turns a page. She watches the carp swim. They're just for decoration. You can't eat them.

"That's where we spend our summer afternoons, watching the shadows climb Father's stone walls, hour by hour, day after day. Persian Geckos watch Sarah while they cling to the inner walls, waiting for her to turn a page. She hardly ever turns a page. She's probably not even reading."

Still, no reaction from Zoe. She stared back, blank as a blonde, blank as a virgin's sugar socket, blank-and-white blank. Why do I bother? I brought her back inside and led her down our spiral staircase. Along the way, I smacked her hand, reminding her to make a fist.

"Our new first floor, as I already mentioned, is really the old second floor, repurposed as entertainment space, where guests are received. Even Uncle Solomon and Auntie Esther are allowed to roam about, eating, drinking, socializing as they please. It's their house, too. But, when guests enter the front door, all of us are honor-bound to feed them, before sending them off." I turned Zoe to face me. "Now, remember,

I'm telling you this because I want you to grasp the nuances of Persian hospitality. Whether entering or leaving, all guests must be accorded the honor and dignity of monarchs, because they are.

"Now you know why the Bulgarians gave us such a large butler's pantry—to assemble trays of delicacies for guests. It's the Persian way. Auntie Esther will probably teach you how to make Persian appetizers served with tea: rice cookies with poppy seeds, chickpea cookies, walnut cookies, cardamom rice cookies, rose water and saffron cookies. Bring a tray up to me if she does. We'll eat some on the terrace.

"To the left of the pantry is an extra-large kitchen. 'But why so large?' you may have asked yourself. Entertaining. It was designed for a natural flow to an even larger gathering room. As part of the family, be prepared to run platters to guests who may be spread all through the house and courtyard.

"Don't be too kind. If you're not careful, you might conduct yourself like a slave girl. Of course, I hope you won't. Such behavior would bring dishonor to our family name. Lately, Uncle Solomon has taken on the demeanor of a servant. I'm not sure why. But, it's very sad.

"Over time, I'll teach you how to exude graciousness, but still inspire fear. Mother often said, 'Think of every appetizer as a gift from the royal kitchen, and you are there to report their response to the king of the house.' You know what I'm saying, like you're in a position of power, and a bad report from you could result in their beheading. Smile, but keep that eagle-eyed look of judgement.

"Opposite the kitchen, on the other side of the formal entry, is Father's library. See the two large oak doors? Pocket doors. They slide open to create a dramatic entrance by Father. I'm about to make an embarrassing confession: Father is a very smart man, but he spells like a gorilla. If he asks you to review his notes, feel free to point out any misspelled words. He likes it. He often brings fellow doctors into the library. They discuss business.

"I suppose that's what they're talking about."

My tiara-wearing Persian princess danced into the gathering room and twirled in ballerina pirouettes. "I've never seen one of your father's parties."

What an emotional punch-in-the-gut. She hadn't. With Mother gone, she probably never would. I'd forgotten how long it had been. Years—two years. I'd forgotten that we may never entertain again. I'd forgotten that Persian manners no longer mattered . . . in this household.

"The spiral staircase is from Spain. It dates back to the 1700s, so it blends exquisitely. Don't you think? At least that's what the Afghan foreman told us. Mother used to pause half-way up, to give us one last reminder before she went to bed. It makes for a lovely departure at the end of an evening . . . until you reach the top. Just bedrooms up there.

"On the bright side, our bedrooms do have reinforced walls. Thick walls stop bullets, but not the heat . . ." I leaned over to whisper in Zoe's ear, ". . . or your sour renditions of *Betty Davis Eyes*."

Zoe's jaw dropped. She pressed her hand over her mouth, hiding her humiliation.

I waggled my head, adding a smirk. "That's right, I hear you.

"Since your bedroom is closest to the terrace, you enjoy a warm winter sun."

"And the killer summer sun," she countered.

I hugged her. "That's why we have the terrace. Step out on the terrace if you can't sleep in this heat. Don't be surprised if you find *me* there.

"The summer stars are spectacular. Just make sure you sleep near the half wall. Stay out of the sight line of the north tower. It would be scandalous if Uncle Solomon watched you sleep. You know, Islamic propriety, and all. And by the way, you sleep about as quiet as an egg beater.

"At any rate, the hallway separates Father's room from ours. His room is gigantic. He has his own steam room and bath. How alone that must make him feel. Never go in there. You know, Islamic propriety and all.

"Sarah calls our side of the hallway, the Silken Corridor. Doesn't that sound pretty?"

Zoe nodded.

"Are you nodding in Bulgarian, or Farsi?"

"Farsi," she said.

"You've probably noticed that Sarah's room is always full of the most beautiful things you can imagine. I'm not sure where she gets everything. Other than school, she hardly ever goes out. She has an expensive painting by Farahnaz Saatchi. I do know where she got that. Father commissioned it for Mother. Saatchi was at the top of his game, and Mother at the peak of her beauty. A match made in art-gallery heaven, but a memory far too painful for Father to keep in his room. And so, to Sarah it went.

"Sarah displays Mother's jewelry. The best pieces hang in shadow boxes, like wall art. I received a few items, but never display them. Unlike Sarah, I hide them.

"Sarah has read books on manners and good conduct, written in the language of the Arabs. I know she turned those pages. Watch her: perfect posture, grace in every step, perfect clothes. Not very fashionable, but clean and neatly pressed.

"But I'm not Sarah. Too many people think we Delkash girls are of the same mind. Not true. I grow flowers and vegetables. That's my role in the family. After Mother died, Father told me: 'Never let a vase be without flowers' . . . and they never are."

I fought back tears and leaned against the dining room wall, averting my eyes. "Since Mother's death, he's afraid of everything. He has an obsessive-compulsive preoccupation with locking gates— MONSTERS, locking doors—BURGLARS, locking seatbelts—SMASHUPS. He locks *everything*. Maybe because he's afraid of dying. 'Who would provide for you girls?' he often complains. That same paranoia sparked compulsory pre-med classes for Sarah and pre-engineering classes for me. You're still too young for *pre*-anything, but that hasn't stopped him from planning. He'll be talking to you about that.

"He'll start dropping hints about marrying well. But, that doesn't include Jews or Christians. Stay away from them. The first Christian church still stands, about fifty miles up the coast. We have over one-hundred-thousand Christians in Iran. That's more than Israel has. Did you know that?"

Zoe shook her head.

Finally, something our little Jew didn't know. I gave her a sideward glare. "Do you like Christians?"

She shrugged.

"Well, as a matter of discretion, it would be best if you said nothing about them. I'm sorry to say this, but the same goes for Jews. The streets crawl with sycophants, anxious to ingratiate themselves to under lords for some imagined political advantage. Who knows how your words could be twisted, knotted and turned. So, zip it up. Do you know what sycophant means?"

She nodded.

That surprised me—disappointed me—because even I had just learned that word. I warned Sarah the day Zoe arrived, *watch this one, she's quick as a mongoose.* "Did you know I openly call you my sister?

Zoe blushed, stretched, twisted, and gazed up with a bashful smile.

"Well, I do. And, you always will be, even if you marry a Jew. Since Sarah rarely leaves the compound,

Father has occasionally taken her to work and made embarrassing introductions to young interns. I can only imagine what humiliations are in store for me. But, little does Father know that I, his future aqua engineer, will be the first to marry—in Paris."

"What?" Zoe's lips curled in disapproval.

"I mean, it's a possibility. That might destroy Father, but I have to go, and not just for love. Since Mother's death, Father sees a sneeze as one step from pneumonia. I would rather die than confess a symptom. I don't like this new side of Father. This Father is weak, afraid, constantly worrying. I dare not encourage those fears. Instead, I nod or shake my head, keeping interchange sparse, waiting for a subject more suited to the dignified Father I remember. And I know he's in there. Given time and encouragement, the old Father is bound to return, strong as ever.

"We're a family in shock, still reeling. Mother was the songbird, the smile, the spirit of our house. In her absence, none of us knew how to fill the void. Father tries, but after two minutes of small talk, out comes his pocket watch, and off he goes, mumbling, leaving the conversation half done.

"Dinner conversations are the worst. I swear, if you hadn't come along with your perky little observations, I don't think we could have made it. I think you amaze Father because of the candor you drag out of him. Thanks be to Allah for your total lack of Islamic propriety. Had you paid scant attention to the mood in the room, you would have stepped back out of respect for our mourning.

"But you didn't.

"And we loved it.

"You ask Father the questions we wouldn't dare.

"Never mind my instructions. Never mind about Islamic propriety and Persian hospitality. You're fine the way you are. You've become a living bridge, connecting angry daughters to a socially inept Father. You're no Mother, but after you arrived, we began to heal. We all felt it. Father speaks to us, through you, and we, likewise, through you to him. Strange, but somehow you've returned the circulation to a dead household. You arrived just in time. With you here, I don't feel so bad about leaving.

"And I am leaving."

Six

Armand is a girl magnet, but so am I . . . no . . . I mean, I'm a boy magnet. It's just that, today, my magnet is working in reverse. I'm following him. Anyway, I trail at a safe distance as he wanders through Azadi Square, toward the Naval Base.

I could burn a forest down with these feelings—feelings desperate to erupt. Volcanic. A cauldron expanding with the fullness of longings, ready to scorch this backward little village.

We Persian women certainly know how to hold our tongues, but when emotions flare, we say it, and say it hot. Maybe Middle-Eastern weather creates residents who feel and respond in ways bizarre to the rest of the world. I'm sure culture and weather connect in some way. Passion has shown me a new thermal landscape (as far as hot things go). I've read that earth has designated hot zones. Lifeforms scrape out existences in the most unlikely places: scalding founts, volcanic islands, and Death Valley (which is in America). I'm sure love has its own means of survival, its preferred host, its ideal temperature, its own law of thermodynamics. Why else would women crave hot baths?

I suppose by most girls' standards, Armand is hot. But he shops more than a woman. I'm sure those are not the right words. *Note to Self: I must think of more masculine ways to describe Armand.*

He passes Gilaneh Restaurant, Ghavamin Bank, Saderat Bank, Mellat Bank, and the Mosque of the Honorable Prophet. Noshahr doesn't have much, but it has plenty of Mosques and banks. A two-pronged marketing plan to fork sinners.

Nancy Drew this: He stops at gold merchants, cologne makers, and Western clothing outlets. Eventually, he stops for another haircut. He gets one twice a week, always in the morning. Seems rather frequent for a man.

Spiritually weak girls swoon at such things. I make it a point to drive them away . . . on behalf of Allah. I feel it's best to establish a twenty-foot barrier, hissing, staring daggers at skanksquatch girls trying to make his acquaintance. It's all I can do to avoid detection. Although, he does glance my way occasionally. I'm sure he thinks it all a coincidence.

I hope he invites me to walk with him, or at least share some local gossip. My heart is singing . . . but no duet. Duets and collaborations. All of nature longs for harmony. Girls are no different. Men need to realize, life is not a solo act. Unity is a potent force, but men don't always see the importance of unifying with a good woman. Find the right woman and watch a man's world transform into a modern-day Paradise. All I'm asking for is a little noticing and a chat or two.

If only Armand would give marital Paradise half a thought, I'm sure he'd start following *me* around. My hydroponic engineering education may not serve his diplomatic aspirations, but show me a file cabinet. I

can file by alphabetical order—and such things.
Someone like me could revolutionize his life. He
should want me.

Iran. Hot for certainties, but all us women get are
rhymes. Always a metaphor; always a clever turn of
phrase; always quoting poets without giving a direct
answer. Give us definitive wedding dates. That's
certainty! Those are the certainties we ache for—as
certain as the sunlight that our sun-loving botany aches
for.

Crape Myrtle trees line our streets. They awaken
at the onset of Iran's mid-day heat. They turn their
leaves up, lifting their branches to give the azure
Middle-Eastern sky an open-mouth kiss. Row after
row blushes with red blossoms of ecstasy. Noshahr—
where every hill has its own story, every valley its own
poem, every girl her own heartache . . . that's for
certain.

So, I continue to pretend-shop at a discreet
distance. I see so many items I desperately want to
buy, but worry Armand will slip away while I haggle.
I'd made that mistake before and lost track of him.
Again, I don't do this often. He just happened by, and
I just happened to notice.

His zig-zag journey has my sense of direction
spinning. Barbershops, gun shops, knife makers—
shops with no pattern or purpose. It's not easy finding
vendors nearby who cater to women. Sometimes, all I
can do is pretend to organize my purse—a Louis
Vuitton.

He spends time in shops unfamiliar to me, in areas I would otherwise avoid. The IRG bunk nearby, inside the Naval Base. Dirty, rude soldiers are common around Azadi Square. Normally, I sidestep this section of town with its uniforms and shops that cater to men's bad habits.

Cut-and-dried monotony.

He turns into a nondescript building, nearly losing me. I push my way through a smelly group of fishermen and find him standing at the end of this dank room . . . urinating.

My neck, face, ears prickle with horror. Soon, I'm a pyre of flame and humiliation.

Public restroom—the *men's* restroom!

I claw my way out, fighting, choking, but manage to keep my dignity, until I end up in lockstep with a row of backward-thinking, burka-wearing women. We look like a line of marching penguins, excluding my bright outfit—a Waad Ali.

Cartoon swoosh cloud: *I could just die!*

I think Armand saw me.

Colonel Sohrabi, the dreaded face of the Guardian Council, appears from nowhere and glares at me, stroking his long beard.

Karmageddon.

Seven

"The person I'm about to introduce you to is twenty-one. Kind of Madonna-old. But, she knows what's happening and how things work." Midday foot traffic at the southern edge of the marketplace was brisk, noisy with happy shoppers, clopping donkey hooves that pulled roughly constructed carts. I hadn't heard one word of appreciation from Giti. So, I turned to command her eye, to force some sort of acknowledgement. "Have you ever wondered where those know-it-alls get all that they know?"

Giti nodded, diffused and distracted by the purses of passing shoppers. With her, gold coins held top priority.

"Well, you're about to find out. Beneath my new friend's headscarf is all you need to know about local social events. She's kind of *cool*, if you understand Western slang. She's the most epically bored person I've ever met, and she likes me. *Me!* Did I mention that she's rich?"

Giti gazed up at the sun-faded sign of the Monkey Bar, then down at me. "Jamileh, why are we here? I thought you were taking me to lunch."

"Lunch, and then some. This place has the cutest side show. Monkey waiters."

"What do they wear?"

"A red vest. No pants. Don't be offended."

"I don't mind. They're just monkeys."

"They have bicycle races, too."

"With your Uncle Solomon?"

"Not people bicycle races, monkey bicycle races. Men will gamble, of course."

"I don't mind," she sniffed. "They're just men."

The orphanage taught their girls religious ritual to the Nth degree, and how to make their own clothes. Giti mended uniforms for the soldiers and even sold a few prayer rugs in the marketplace. *Self-sufficiency* they called it.

Ha!

I sized her up and got this sick feeling that she was about to ruin everything. Giti never missed an opportunity to show up her superiors. I stopped dead in my tracks and patted her down for a hidden prayer rug. No religious drama was too outrageous for her.

I reached up to adjust her cheap polyester headscarf—saffron. Then I brushed the dust from the shoulders of her unpressed cotton abaya—saffron—again. It was nice enough. "There. Now, act natural.

"No, not like that." I pressed my hand against her spine to straighten her posture.

"Before we go inside, permit me to review a few rules. A monkey will act as your waiter, but the one writing your order will be the Russian hostess, standing behind him. The hostess will only say two Farsi words: *Order Coke*. How they manage to make those happy words sound so hateful I'll never know. It won't take long to discover: monkeys, fun; Russian hostesses, irksome. The only actual work the monkeys do is deliver bottles of Coke to your table. You can send anything back if you're not completely satisfied."

For the first time Giti smiled. "I won't send anything back. I love monkeys. Are we allowed to feed them?"

"No. And don't touch them."

She leaned toward the entrance and sighed. "I just want to pet one."

"No. Don't touch the monkeys."

After we entered, the door closed behind us with a *thud*. The entrance hall was dark. We swayed and groped for a wall, anything to prevent us from tipping over. We stood, frozen in place, waiting for our eyes to adjust. This must have overwhelmed Giti, because she gripped my shoulders with both hands. I placed my hands on her hips to reassure her . . . and prevent her from running outside.

Voices of village idiots roiled in a jester's stew of odds-making tomfoolery. Occasionally, a monkey screamed in the heat of competition, and crude words were freely spoken. The more sophisticated were forced to tolerate such low-minded displays.

After my eyes adjusted, I led Giti further inside. A constant cloud of sweet smoke, tobacco, incense, and hashish hung overhead. Most of the village boys stood around the racetrack, which looked like a huge oval-shaped bowling alley—minus the pins.

Giti elevated that pious nose of hers. "It smells like monkeys. I can almost see monkey dander in the air. Wouldn't want it on my food. This place is anything but *halal*."

I decided to brighten her up with a tour. I veered toward the back, where the top racers prepare for their turn on the track. "Meet Bosco," I said. "He's the champion rider."

Giti grabbed my arm and moaned. "He looks so sad."

"He's not like the other racers. He's a prisoner *and* a racer. He's glum because he's in love with Orange Peel. She lives at the Zoo, but they keep Bosco here, under house arrest. Chimpanzees are like men. They can spot beauty a mile away. They just know.

"In any case, Bosco was wild, a street monkey, and Orange Peel was tame, raised in the zoo. They used to slip out at night, until Bosco was falsely accused of biting a god-fearing woman on the arse.

"The real perpetrator of the arse bite was Shin Bone, Armand's pet chimp."

Giti's head bobbed with slow nods. "Well, there you go. Armand's a weasel-of-a-man, determined to avoid responsibility at any cost."

"Giti! We're just talking about monkeys. Anyway, Shin Bone was supposed to be a racer, but when he showed little aptitude, Armand's dad sold Shin Bone to the Zoo. Now, Shin Bone lives with Orange Peel, Bosco's woman.

"Such a sad story.

"It's forbidden to bite a woman's arse. In the absence of a legal precedent, the Imams decided to apply human law to the guilty monkey, whoever it turned out to be. They narrowed it down to Bosco or Shin Bone. The victim was unable to distinguish one monkey from the other.

"Some said Armand trained Shin Bone to do *his* bidding, that Shin Bone only did as he was trained. So technically, Armand should have gotten the life sentence in some monkey cage."

Giti smirked, as if vindicated.

I put my hands on my hips and glared her into submission. "I shame anyone who dares repeat this unfounded accusation." I blinked hard to put an emotional period at the end of my sentence. "But Armand's dad, being the ambassador to France, used his influence to protect Armand's chimp. So, here sits poor Bosco, locked up at the Monkey Bar, forced to race bicycles all day. A sordid affair, to say the least."

Giti took one step back. "How do you know all of this?"

"Uncle Solomon. Occasionally, he and Bosco train together."

Giti stepped forward until we were nose to nose. "Can you just let that sink in for a moment? Are you saying *Bosco* told your Uncle Solomon?"

The question stopped me cold. "I don't know. I hadn't thought about it." I stood there scratching my head. At some point in our conversation, I'm sure Uncle Solomon must have mentioned how he came by the information, but, I racked my brain and couldn't recall what it was. "He often drives by the zoo. He probably spoke to one of the zoo keepers. Anyway, since Bosco became the champion racer, he wasn't exterminated." Yet, Giti's question persisted in the back of my mind. "I too wondered how Uncle Solomon came by his information, and why Armand hadn't explained everything to the Basij."

I looked at Bosco and wished he could fill in the blanks. He even leaned forward, eyes watering, mouth open. I sensed he wanted to tell me something. His eyes beckoned, like he was on the verge of imparting an important detail.

Bosco's intensity frightened me—not to mention, the awful memory of him flicking his cigarette at me. I backed away, but continued explaining everything to Giti. "Someday I'll ask Armand why he didn't intervene. After all, he's majoring in International Law. He's a Master Debater."

"A what!"

"Master Debater, d-e-b-a-t-e-r."

"Oh, I thought you said something else."

"Anyway, that was that. The Imams made sure Bosco took the fall for the whole arse-biting spree."

Giti was no longer paying attention to a word I said. "He's waving to you."

"Who?" I asked.

"You. See. He's still waving at you."

My head swiveled in Bosco's direction. Indeed, he was signing a bewildered farewell, barely bending his monkey fingers in a lackluster *goodbye*.

Giti shifted restlessly. "You said you had a job for me. What do you want me to do?"

She never listens. "I said, I *know* someone who *might* have a job for you. Ava Herat."

She made such a horrific sneer I feared her face would break. "I know Ava. She's a pimp with a fake French accent."

That set me back. I couldn't imagine someone from Giti's social strata knowing someone like Ava. "She is no such thing. And I won't have you embarrassing me in front of my new friends. A woman of her means could always use a good seamstress. So, I expect nothing but good manners from you."

"I'll try." Giti turned her back to me.

Hardly a convincing defense. I spun her around to face me. "Even if you and Ava don't get to Yahtzee, don't forget about lunch. You could still drink an American Coca-Cola and eat a falafel. You can even bet on the races."

"I'm an orphan. People like me don't enjoy such leisure. We don't play golf or gamble."

Giti was a nice girl, but every now and then, she zinged me with her orphan shtick. I swallowed my anger. *Okay*, I told myself, *I'll just side-step all that.*

"Can I feed some of my falafel to the monkeys?" she asked, again.

"Don't touch the monkeys. It's the rule."

Out in the audience, a single shaft of light cut through the smoke and shone down on Ava's table. There she sat, bored with life itself. Well dressed, trendy as ever. Her clothing was a clever dodge of Islamic modesty. She'd covered herself in all the right places, but stood out in bold contrast to the other women—audaciously tailored—unapologetically gorgeous. Her headscarf was milk-white, but she wore a hooded abaya of camel-brown. The two-tone sensation showed every artful stitch of its masterful designer. So understated. Ava was a textile canvas that highlighted her David Yurman custom jewelry. *Stunning.*

"This feminine billboard of Middle-Eastern fashion stopped me on the street last month. She ran her hand over the seam of my jilbab, admiring the color and fabric. She only said a few words. 'We are living in a gender-quake, a modern sexodus. We have a duty to project dis female revolution in da way we dress. Come visit me at da Monkey Bar and tell me who tailors your outfits.' She's been my fashion role model ever since.

"I thought I knew everyone in Noshahr, but how pleasantly wrong I was. Ava has introduced me to people from all manner of profession and station—upper stations, of course."

Giti rolled her eyes and refused to look.

I gulped and stared in admiration. Ava was a living fashion poster. More amazing than anything in my fashion magazines, yet culturally appropriate.

As usual, Ava was at the center of everything. "Take note, Giti, everyone in the Monkey Bar eventually circles by her table to pay tribute. Even the girls from the balcony."

Giti squirmed and grumbled. "Yeah, well, they're whores. They have to."

I felt sorry for Ava. There was just no way to get on Giti's good side. I took Giti by the hand and gave it a stern shake. "Mature pill! She could be your ticket out of the orphanage."

Eight

"Salaam, Ava," I said in my most delightful voice. People often comment on how nice I am.

"Salaam, Jamileh," she replied, as she gave Giti a double-dose of skunk eye.

Giti half-raised one arm in thinly disguised hostility, a wave more feeble than Bosco's *goodbye*.

After we sat, Ava glared sidelong at Giti. "Sorry I slap you last week, but I did not tink you would ever stop talking, and I had somewhere to go." Then, with a quick toss of her head, "Bad day."

Some people have described Ava as religiously non-observant, but I think she's starved for love. She must have been deprived in her youth. That's why she acts out. Deep down, she didn't have a good opinion of herself. Not that she's perfect. I just think she could use a hug.

Giti, however, was less broadminded. "Was it really a bad day, Ava, or did you have a bad five minutes that you milked all day?"

Ava leaned back until her shoulders met the chair's top rail, her head swayed like a cobra before striking. I got a bad feeling my welcome was about to be revoked.

A slight, but devilish smirk crossed Ava's face. "Sure babe. I'll hit shuffle . . . since you are wid da good doctor's daughter."

Maybe Giti could use a little more rescuing than she realized. I wasn't sure if Giti would ever find work in our village. "Ava, this might be a bad time, an unfortunate imposition, but I would consider it a personal favor if you would find respectable work for my friend, Giti. She will soon be seventeen, and she'll have to leave the orphanage. Without meaningful work, or a beneficial marriage, her life could take a bad turn."

Although my words were temperate and well-expressed, they seemed to repulse Ava. My timing has never been precise. Ava regarded me the way a widow spider examines a housefly. She laughed loudly, a vulgar Occidental laugh, the laugh of a person who wraps their next meal in silk before draining their lifeblood. But, I have been known to imagine things.

"You certainly amuse. Such a smart girl. You use dat mout of yours like a tommy gun, rat-a-tat-tat. *Ouf.*"

I raised both palms. "Don't answer today. Think about it. These matters have a way of resolving themselves. A loyal hardworking girl like Giti could become an important pillar in your household. This is all serendipity. I'm sure of it."

Ava chuckled dismissively as she scanned the room, unimpressed and distracted. She exhaled with great drama and eventually made conversation with someone standing behind her.

Swerve.

Eviction day at the orphanage loomed large over Giti—and I worried deeply for her. "Allah will provide," I whispered. But Giti rolled her eyes, unconvinced.

The words had barely crossed my lips when heavy steps advanced toward our table. A boorish laborer of some type emerged from a crowd of timid Coke-drinking men. He moved toward us with the wide menacing stance of a wrestler, black glistening hair, jutting like straight shards from beneath a Pashtun cap. Strong as an acre of garlic.

He stared at me with an undignified glimmer that I wished wasn't there. I'm no proctologist, but this whiffy had *ass* written all over his forehead.

He faced Ava, but his eyes kept cutting back toward me. His five dirty fingers hovered just above our table, dropping a small stack of gold coins.

Ava shook her head.

I'm sure I heard a sprinkling of laughter from the crowd. In a shiver of anger he snatched up his coins, and left. He still lingered nearby, staring at me, mumbling, with his dreadfully ordinary friends.

What force Ava held over this Neanderthal was a mystery to me. I suppose she did me a favor, but nothing was mentioned. Yet, I sensed Ava's protection at work. The Monkey Bar could be an unsettling place, the sort of place one needed a guardian—or a derringer. After my breathing returned to normal, I leaned toward Ava, within whisper distance. "Have you seen Armand?"

"He's here," she said with an exasperated sigh.

I should have been more discreet, but I jumped up, nearly knocking my chair over. I scanned the room from one side to the other. I noticed a simmering disgust from Ava. She had already lectured me about reserve—a woman's most powerful weapon.

Ugh.

Ava's right. I should master this feminine aloofness thing, but proper or not, I continued looking. I adjusted my headscarf further back on my head to show just enough hair, to give me the look of daring. I wanted Armand to think of me as edgy, mature, an uninhibited woman.

I covered my mouth and whispered into Giti's ear. "Friend card."

"I'm here," she said with a ready nod.

"Be my divine bridle. Armand is here—somewhere."

"So?"

"I don't trust myself. You may need to rein this filly in. He moves me to madness. He's an indescribable poetic impression. He's Persian blood re-defined by Parisian culture, softened in the right places, yet, fierce where it counts. Dreamy. The kind of boy you can't get too close to, because you might get lost in his brown eyes and melancholy."

"Armand?" Giti shivered, critical as ever. "He hangs out with all those cologne-drenched losers, draped in South African gold, wearing tight Western trousers. Economic traitors." Giti crinkled her nose, as if I'd missed something. "He may not even be alive by the end of the month. He turned eighteen." She wagged her head to make the point I missed. "Mandatory armed service!"

I felt the blood drain from my face. I'd never thought of Armand as someone bound by the same laws as underprivileged boys. My eyes must have frightened Giti, because she covered her mouth, leaning, leaning, leaning away.

"Don't look at me like that," Giti said. "You know the law."

"What do I know about army stuff?" Angry, my volume broke free. "And I can't be held responsible for what my face does." If our eyes locked, I knew I'd strike her in a fit of rage—probably with a hard knuckle. I turned my chair away and refused to face her. I needed to regain my composure. I thought Giti was my friend. The snake that bites is always the one you didn't see.

I gathered my resolve, determined to keep my word. I would buy Giti's lunch. Then, if Ava and Giti would excuse me, I'd find Armand and exchange a few words. *Oh, my dear Armand. What will this war do to you?*

Women have more love receptors than men. People cringe when I say that, but dogs smell things humans can't perceive; birds chart courses by a force that has no pull on women. Why can't women feel things that men can't? *How about that?* I challenged my imaginary detractors.

Ava grabbed my hand beneath the table. Her head rocked toward someone behind me. Armand.

"*Bonjour*, Armand," I said, almost a yell.

Armand was slow to turn, but when our eyes met I watched his face come to life with a warm smile. Armand bowed deeply, touching the fingers of his right hand to his lips, then to his forehead, a Middle-

Eastern cliché of respect. "Salaam, daughter of Islam. Cruised any public restrooms lately?"

So, he *had* seen me.

Every fiber of my being hoped he hadn't. But, I had no intention of dignifying his question with a response . . . and besides, Ava watched me like a desert hawk.

"So, what brings you to the Monkey Bar?" he asked.

Ah, dialogue I could participate in. "Entertainment. Show business is my life. Go ahead, ask me anything about show business." I discreetly sucked in my cheeks, hoping he would mention my astounding resemblance to Anicee Alvina.

Armand folded his arms, accepting the challenge. "Who was the female lead in *You've Got Mail*?"

I realized I'd created a persona I could never live up to. "I meant Middle-Eastern show business. Go ahead, ask me anything about Middle-Eastern show business." Again, cheeks tastefully sucked in.

"Who was the female lead in *Downpour*?"

"Please, I have no interest in weather." If only we had an automatic television, I'm sure I'd do better at this game.

"Who was the female lead in *White Balloon*?"

By this time, I had lost all my enthusiasm for sucking my cheeks in. "What I *meant* to say, Animal Entertainment. Veterinary Medicine is my life, a big part of my life."

His eyes sparkled, as though about to pounce. "What kind of animals have you raised?"

"So far, chickens. That's why I come here. I want to understand the monkey: how they think; what motivates them; what they can teach us, stuff such as that."

"The marketplace is full of exotic animals, from all parts of the world. Why the Monkey Bar?"

"Primates. I'm drawn to the suborder of haplorhini." I'd heard Sarah use that word.

Giti kicked my leg beneath the table. I turned in her direction. She was pulling back with both hands, attempting to rein me in.

"And what have you learned?" asked Armand.

Drat. Every question turned into an interrogation. Why couldn't we talk about celebrations, marital engagements, or weather? I love the weather! "Feast your eyes on the track," I said. "Isn't it nice to see all those happy monkey faces? How fun to watch another version of us riding the bicycle."

Armand grinned, but showed no sign of agreement.

"In times past, Noshahr had an organ grinder," I said in a louder voice. "When the Basij arrived, he left us for Azerbaijan. I remember him winding that magical wooden box of music while his monkey danced for coins. Remember?"

"Those were different times," Giti said. "We had kites, balloons, and Gypsies."

Determined to keep the spotlight on myself, I raised my voice. "I just thought it strange that when monkeys play, we laugh. Why do we laugh?" I pointed, again, to the race track. "Their joy gives us joy. You would think a man would invest the same effort in his wife's happiness. Shouldn't a good husband make his wife laugh? Wouldn't that make for an infectiously joyous home?"

Armand's arms unfolded. Something I said captured his attention. I didn't exactly know which words did the trick, but I was glad I diverted his thoughts from war—assuming war was what preoccupied his thoughts.

He turned toward the track, distracted by the metallic clatter of bicycles preparing for the next race. "Poor little fellows. But, a man must gamble on something," he said, as a diversion to whatever stabbed at him, earlier.

I probed deeper. "We're all coping—monkeys and humans." How stupid I sounded, digging yet another hole. "I mean, I noticed Bosco is a chain smoker. Now, there's a bad habit to break." My goodness, at last, a true statement. "What compels a primate to display oral transference? And 'transference' is a psychological term, you know," I said with the raised brow of an expert.

Giti made a face at me that meant—*what?*

"What is *your* diagnosis, Dr. Delkash?" asked Armand.

This was the longest conversation I'd ever had with Armand. I was near fainting, a heady out-of-body experience. I planned to discuss how Bosco needed a wife, but somehow got sucked into this silly smoking discussion. Why couldn't I shut up?

"My diagnosis? I imagine Bosco remembers how he was taken into captivity. He was probably torn from his dead mother's breast. I lost my mother too. I understand his pain. We're both coping."

Yes!

Did I just sound smart? I think so. I looked around the table for support. Everyone was nodding, even Ava, and she's a tough crowd. Armand was the only one standing, but he too began to nod.

"Are you Sarah's sister?" he asked.

I nodded.

"Yes, I heard about your mother," he said. "I'm sorry for your loss."

I had long since tired of condolences. "Thank you."

"How is Sarah handling the loss?" he asked.

"I spend my time consoling these poor monkeys, but in reality, maybe I'm sorting out my own pain. Sarah volunteers at the orphanage. That's how she copes. Father puts his heart into pancreatic research. Zoe never misses an opportunity to console me and Sarah, that's how she copes. What pathetic primates we are, all broken and sad."

"Who is Zoe?" asked Armand.

"Zoe?" Uh-oh, how careless of me. Muslims don't adopt. Loose talk like that could trigger a visit from the Secret Police. Giti was the only person at our table who knew of Zoe's Jewish origins.

Giti: my only mamluk, janissary, safeguard, my shield between honor and social stigma. I gave her my shut-the-hell-up face, but publicly, I barely shook my head, just enough to scare her into silence.

Then, I pertly lifted my head toward Armand and smiled. "She's . . . uh . . . my youngest sister."

Nine

Like the Sword of Damocles, conscription loomed large over Armand's head. Time raced much too fast for him, but had the opposite effect on me.

Minute by agonizing minute I lived in slow motion. Dinner dragged on and on. I was always on the verge of saying something, but never sure how it would be received. Dinner with Father always gave me a nervous stomach.

Four at the table, and one empty chair. Sarah filled one chair, but lived in a world apart, her busy mind playing over her pre-med studies. Father's thoughts were his, and his alone. All I thought about was Paris—and poor Armand.

It occurred to me, I had no idea what went through Zoe's mind, or what she did while I was at the Monkey Bar. I suppose she read my fashion magazines, plundered my makeup, worshipped Jehovah? Maybe she hung out with Auntie Esther? I'd really never thought about it. A case could be made that I'd been living in an alternate Jamilehverse.

Until Zoe arrived, I was adrift, alone, brooding. Desperate to converse, desperate to share, desperate for comradery. In a complaining house of women, Zoe was the only stair that didn't creak. But, relying on a thirteen-year-old girl had its limits.

"Who unlatched the doors last night?" Father asked—again—as he did every night.

I bit my tongue, but it was me. I unlatched everything, so I could breathe. Confinement stole my breath and pressed like lead weights against my chest.

Insanity depends on perspective, that is, who had locked who in what. I'm insane. I'll admit that too. I have that awful condition: cleithrophobia. Father knew all of this, of course, but nowadays he never asks direct questions.

I was determined to show him the world outside should be invited in—celebrated. I had every intention of doing the same thing tomorrow, and all nights thereafter, until he conceded, or, I made my escape to *gay Paree*.

Father wiped his mouth with his linen napkin, rose from the table as if to yell and rampage. I didn't care. Maybe I would finally see passion in that lifeless face of his. Any emotion would be an improvement. Instead, he went out to the courtyard to secure our compound's huge cedar gate.

Clack!

I flinched at the sound of the iron bolt smashing against its iron latch. Most homes are about the same size as an animal enclosure. I've visited my share of zoos. Like caged monkeys, me, Sarah, and Zoe, waited at the dining room table for our keeper.

Maybe he was honor-bound to lock us in, by some imagined duty? Perhaps this was an Islamic preparation to make us contented wives? Were these locks supposed to dampen useless dreams that sparked needless desires? Or, was he a mad man, sick and demented?

Woman: the last animal to be civilized by man.

We ran to the dining room window and watched Father zig-zag through the courtyard, executing his sad evening ritual: secure the outer gate; check the garage door from inside the carriage house; check the security bars on the ground-floor windows; lock the outer doors of the house from the inside; and finally, join his three little monkeys for dinner.

He returned to his dining room chair. *Rrrrr!* Even the sound of his sliding chair grated on my already raw nerves. He ate, head down, stabbing at his food. The *clinks* from his knife and fork against chinaware were unendurable.

Click, clang, grind, zing, clap, schlik. Racket, racket, racket.

Every sound he made rattled through my mind, touting its resistance to change. Like it or not, the Basij ruled our streets. Like it or not, Mohammad Reza was out of power. Like it or not, Mother was gone. Father's old world was gone, but I wanted to live, to laugh.

I knew something shiny was calling Iran's youth. I could never specify its point of origin. I could never make out its shape, but I recognized its voice. *Over here!* I always responded. But, an unpredictable stretch of time elapsed between its calls. For reasons beyond me, I could never locate it, and it never carried me away to freedom.

"Eat," Father barked, pointing to my plate.

That's just the kind of thing that makes me crazy. I'm not hungry for food. I'm starving for conversation.

Since Mother's passing, dinners have been ruined by his fear to move on. One day she was gone, like smoke. Since then, we'd been tied in every emotional knot you could imagine, yet never saying that awful word—*dead*.

Such conversations were discreetly avoided. After dinner, Father secluded himself in the library, just him and a hookah pipe. Hashish and solitude finished his evenings, and by extension, ours. I often heard sobs through the library door.

We all had.

Here it came: Father tossed his napkin on the table and excused himself, abandoning his family for another smoking bowl of self-pity. I suppose a man smokes to slow down the ever downward spiral of his life . . . or at least confronting it. Good riddance. Never had a man left a room with so little impact.

Zoe, to my great surprise, jumped up and grabbed his hand, pulling him away from the library. "I know you don't feel like you have any fight left, but find it—for us. If you're concrete, rigorous, and prescriptive, anything is possible."

Father froze, speechless. He had never struck Zoe before, but the way he looked down at her, I couldn't tell what would happen next. His brows furrowed, lips tightened.

At long last, he fell to his knees and hugged little Zoe at the waist, sobbing.

Sarah ran to them and dropped to her knees, then in some catatonic slow-motion blur, I too knelt and hugged Father.

We cried, looking into each other's faces and cried some more. Sometimes, forgiveness breaks your shackles, sets you free from emotional bondage.

My burdens lifted away, like white balloons on their way to God.

This is it.

We've finally turned the corner.

I have no idea what lays ahead, this is new ground.

In this joyous bond, we hug, apologize, and swear our love until poor Zoe, the only one standing, staggers, pushing us away, desperate to sit.

"Please, take a seat, girls," Father says, wiping his damp eyes. He walks into the pantry and brings out a jug of wine.

Wine? Are we not Muslims! Alcohol is forbidden. All us girls look at each other, in shock.

"This is not for drinking." His voice is hoarse, as if rising through cobwebs. "This is for celebrating, swearing vows, making oaths." He goes to the cabinet and retrieves four silver chalices. He pours a small amount in each, about four-fingers in depth, and takes a seat.

A cold chill sweeps through every chamber of my heart. I fear he's about to ask us to drink. I am *certain* he intends to ask us to drink.

He raises his chalice, with one hand over his heart. "Never more. Never more. Never more. The dark days that cast a pall over this house are gone. Love will live here. From this day forward," his volume dips to a whisper, "love will live here." And down his throat went the wine in only a few gulps.

Then, without hesitation, little Zoe grabs her chalice with both hands and throws her head back until it's empty. A few coughs later, she plops her cup atop the table. She's either a genius or a drunkard, I'm not sure which. To my horror, Sarah drinks hers.

Emboldened, I grab my chalice and drink it all—with only a few pauses in-between. How odd. Minus the burn, it has a familiar taste, a very putrid grapey taste. Not at all satisfying . . . but the ritual is.

Here I sit, our pact made. The four of us are human again, part of a defiant tribe. As I look around the table we all have huge grins—and a little zaniness in our eyes. I must admit, it is a diabolical ceremony—wicked and exciting. How shall I describe it? We're like Western Christians, born again, but without nailing our God to a cross. All our tomorrows will be . . . different.

Father's metaphorical windows of possibility are finally open, showing us what the world outside really looks like. Infinite. Which is good, because inquisitiveness withers behind locked doors. Tonight, tears have finally opened Father's eyes. Then, two years of misery crumble into a thousand manageable pieces, like a pomegranate emptying itself of delicious little revelations.

Alexander the Great entered Persia and named our seasonal winds. It seems we've mourned at least that long—centuries. Now, we can wade into the aftermath of our long-awaited healing.

Sooner or later, families must learn that we are all in this together. We all make it, or none of us will. For us, we're making it, no spite, no grudges. Our eyes clear, our hearts softened. I want everyone to feel what we feel, and know what we know. I want to proclaim, *there is peace in surrender*.

Father shoots from his chair laughing out loud. "And that is that. Flee from this home you devils of sorrow! Good riddance misery." He pounds the cork back in the wine jug and returns it to whatever secret place he had taken it from. Thanks to Zoe, he stepped out of the pantry relaxed, at peace, and for the first time in two years, happy.

He carefully closes the pantry door—precisely. But he doesn't return to his chair. He goes out our front door, toward the gate. Again, grinding iron shatters my peace.

Clack!

Father is re-checking the latch on the front gate—scelerophobia. His psychosis contends with mine—scelerophobia vs. cleithrophobia. I flinch at the sound of iron smashing against iron. Has he forgotten? He made his security check less than an hour earlier.

He re-secures our front door—again.

Not everything has changed. Maybe nothing has changed. I stare at the silver chalice in front of me. It stares back, laughing at me. It tells me I've sinned, and

the spot of red at the bottom is evidence. It tells me
that not even iron bars can protect me from the bitter
consequences of apostasy. It banishes me from our
table, from our house, from our village, from Islam.

I could fill an ox cart with all I long for; more
attention from Armand; a second chance with Mother;
a do-over with Father—and I never, never, should
have drank that nasty wine. It was probably Zoe's
Passover wine.

I suppose change means different things to
different people.

Change is so hard.

Ten

Father and I sat in the back of the *Monstrosity*. I noticed that Uncle Solomon's eyes watched us from his rear-view mirror. His eyes shaky-jumped from the road ahead back to Father. Something about Father had Uncle Solomon on edge.

"Doctor?" Uncle Solomon queried, overawed and whispery.

I too had noticed Father's ponderous thousand-mile stare. I worried about the consequences of last night's alcohol. Both of us were on edge, worried about Father, the winebibber, the apostate.

"Dr. Delkash?" Uncle Solomon repeated, this time with more blare.

Gradually, Father's mind re-engaged. His eyes gleamed like wet berries.

"Are you all right?" Uncle Solomon asked.

Father's smile came slow, but eventually matched the glint in his eyes. "Solomon. I'm sorry. You were saying something?"

"No sir. We have not spoken since breakfast. I just wanted to let you know we are about five minutes from your office."

Father's spine straightened, his eyes incredulous. He cranked his window down and checked the road signs, as if to gather his bearings. At forty miles per hour, the wind blew his fedora into my lap. He cranked the window up and replaced his hat. "No, no, that won't do. Drop me off at the Gardens. I'll need a walk before starting my rounds." His head dipped, ever so solemn. "We've lost so many this week. Persian pride. I'm afraid it's killing us."

"Who?" I asked. "Who's killing us?"

"Not who. It. Politics. We can't transfer patients out of Iran and can't bring foreign doctors in. No one in, no one out, and those who cross illegally face severe consequences. Yet, wounded soldiers continue to pour in from the Naval Infirmary.

"If I had a larger staff, I could manage. But with the Iraq Border War, U.N. embargoes, and our ban on foreign interns— well, it's bad. Really bad."

The war—always the war. No wonder Armand dropped out of school. The poor boy was self-medicating with gambling and parties. Precious Armand. "What happened? What were the 'severe consequences' for those who crossed illegally?"

"I don't know." Father scratched at his goatee. "A few young nurses tried their midnight escape and we never heard from them again."

I wasn't scared. None of this would stop me. *Oh dear Allah, protect my journey to Paris.* "I bet you miss Zoe's father," I said, intentionally changing the subject. "He was *my* favorite intern."

"More than you know." His right hand balled into a quivering fist. "If I hadn't recruited him, Zoe would still have her father."

I leaned away, avoiding his brimming anger.

"If I hadn't recruited Dr. Mousa, Israel would still have a fine endocrinologist." Father let it all go with a shake of his head.

I hadn't worked out the dates and details, but Sarah and I knew the murder of Zoe's parents troubled Father. As I watched, I realized how deeply he blamed himself. I'm not sure why. He has enough problems without searching for more. Noshahr has a never-ending supply of broken bodies and Father never turns anyone away.

But good intentions can't overcome a broken system. Medical couriers were always delivering the wrong thing, too late, for patients beyond recovering. He had confided all this to us in clinical jargon, but behind the cold medical terminology we sensed his dismay.

Uncle Solomon passed the hospital heading toward Father's new destination, Noshahr's Botanical Gardens. We continued down Satarkhan Road. He turned right at Café Salar. Halfway, we approached a scraggly group of Revolutionary Guards, leaning against the back wall of a silversmith. The wall behind them had a fresh message: *10,000 Kurdish rebels, unavailable for comment.* Spray painted by one of those ringworm-infested soldiers, no doubt. They were big on murdering harmless Kurdish farmers, but avoided Russian pirates on the Caspian. The Kurds were defenseless; the pirates were well armed. Such brave soldiers.

I winced at Father's lack of revulsion.

He smiled and gave my hand a reassuring grip. "Iranians are, at heart, good people. Normally, they incline toward inscrutability when it comes to political stances. They may complain about high prices, or peacock over the shortcomings of neighbors, but they've always judiciously hid their political discontent." Then, as we passed, he shook his fedora angrily at the soldiers. "But this, this is new, painting graffito, ghostly at its edges."

The soldiers alerted to Father's gesturing. I restrained him. A bullet was never far away from such confrontations.

Father stared into the distance, cow eyed. "What are we to do?" He fidgeted, turning his hat, round and round, as his mouth twitched. "I once read that an American abolitionist wept, 'If I had convinced more slaves that they were slaves, I could have freed thousands more.'"

This was a side of Father I hadn't seen before. He *was* upset. Maybe our after-dinner vows had meant something.

"I'm ashamed," he said. "We Iranians are shells of what we used to be. Half Iran is no longer Persian. A patchwork of neighborhoods spreads through this once unified nation: Sunni Muslims from Saudi Arabia, Wahhabi Muslims from Qatar, Shiite Muslims from Iraq, Sufi Muslims from Turkey, Bahai Muslims from India. What are we becoming? What were we? I suppose it's all a myth. When has anyone ever been one of anything?" He spoke these things barely above a whimper. "I don't care anymore. Stay here long enough and you won't either."

That perked my ears up. "We should leave!"

He laughed. "You're a bit too anxious. All good things come to the patient. Solomon will soon be off to the Olympics with his bicycle racing. In a few years, I'll be sending Sarah to study abroad—London. You won't be far behind."

Such talk. It sounded like Father was clearing the deck for something big—sending us away to protect us from the consequences of some secret plan. Maybe he was saving my life from these soldiers-of-the-spray-can. Maybe he could see something over the horizon that I couldn't.

I was more than willing to go, but something was wrong. For one thing, after we passed Café Salar, Father dropped a wad of cash in Uncle Solomon's lap without counting out the denominations. Whatever haunted Father, I hoped a wad of cash would turn up in my not-too-distant future.

"I've been asked to sit on the City Council," he said abruptly, eyes darting here and there, almost guilty about it.

Why do old men gravitate toward politics? It's the hot stove that every fool must touch. "Is that like a politician?" I asked.

"Not exactly, but it does come with civic duties . . . political in nature. I guess doctors are always searching for a disease. Bad politics is as good as any. That too needs treatment, prescribed and administered."

"Think," Uncle Solomon interrupted, "this could be a good omen, a healthy step forward. You will move in new circles, meet new people. Who knows, maybe a good woman is in need of a good man."

I could hardly believe my ears. Mother rescued Uncle Solomon, and now *this*. "Father is certainly in no position for marriage," I snapped. "It's only been two years."

Father's shoulders folded in slightly, and a disturbing grin appeared. "Emil Hussein was a widower. He formed marriage three months after his wife passed. I'm no Emil, but maybe a woman in the house would be good for my daughters."

"Oh, so that's it," I responded, icy and shrill. "Well, in case you were wondering: No, we don't need a new mother."

Father put his hat in the back window and gave me a hug. It was a long and uncomfortable hug. "Nor do I need a new wife. But we need something different. Don't we?"

I nodded.

He held me by my shoulders at arm's length and smiled broadly. "Your mother can't be replaced, and I wouldn't try. My goodness . . . what a woman. I've seen her in a room full of quarreling neighbors, and whatever thin membrane of commonality that joined them, she found. She moved among them like a water strider, without disturbance, conveying words from one side of the idea-world to the other, smiling all the while.

"How she found such middle ground I'll never know. But I learned a few things by watching her. Maybe I can pass that along—help someone."

That was rich. He barely kept up with his hours at the hospital. "Politics will survive without you. Besides, diplomacy comes at a cost. I saw how it drained Mother, and now I see how Sarah avoids neighbors. Other people's squabbles exhausted Mother. I think it played a role in her failing health. And if you dabble in politics, it'll ruin your health too."

People like Mother are rare, smooth as glass, but easily fractured. Noshahr is less bearable without her. I've noticed the hunger in everyone's eyes, hoping Sarah will replace her.

I'm sure that's why Sarah rarely goes out. It must be a heavy mantle to bear. Maybe it's unfair, but I too nudge her in that direction. I have to. I'm one of the few people who gets to talk to her. Hint by hint, thread by thread, Sarah is coming along, like a fine Persian carpet. *But Father?*

Uncle Solomon parked in front of the Botanical Gardens. Father, anxious to leave, put his hat on, swung his door open and stepped out. Before reaching for his medical bag, he searched his pockets and came up with one of Mother's rings, one I hadn't seen in years. He pushed it at me, until I took it.

"Jamileh . . . you and Sarah are more alike than you realize. Sarah hyper-matured physically. You hyper-matured intellectually. Both gifts will create mistaken perceptions by outsiders. People will mistake you for being older than you are. That, my little chatterbox, will be a never-ending fountain of awkward situations. Beware. Intelligence does not equal maturity. Intelligence does not equal wisdom."

A long pause ensued. I avoided his eyes and stared, instead, at the ring. The silence between us stretched—strained.

"I love you, Jamileh."

"I know."

"It's okay if you don't love me."

"I love you," I lied.

"No, you don't. But it's okay. Our God requires a child to *honor* their parent, and you've lived up to that. You keep our home in fresh flowers. You welcome me home with special treats—lemon-herb chicken, rose-petal tea. I notice. God requires that you *love* Him, *love* the stranger, but the father only merits *honor*. I'm telling you this so you won't torture yourself. There's no need to feel guilty."

"I told you, I *do* love you." I had no idea what was making Father behave so strange, but he was starting to annoy me.

"Not in your tone, not in your expression, not in your heart. Don't worry. Sometimes, I think you need permission. I hereby give it. I have enough love for all of us. If I have done my job, as a parent, your natural adolescent chemistry will cause you to rebel against me, thus allowing you to be attracted to a good man. It's a natural part of growing up."

"*Ew*, Dad! Could we drop this?"

He just stood there, with a hokey grin. "You will love him. He will be yours and you will be his. But I will always love you, and your new family can always depend on me. That's all I wanted to say. I only hope you make it through these difficult years without destroying your future. And it's so, so, easy to destroy your future."

"Stop it! I won't destroy my future."

Father grabbed his bag, blew me a kiss, and shut the door. I lowered my head and refused to look up until I could no longer hear the *crunch* beneath his gravely steps.

Uncle Solomon pulled away. "Monkey Bar? I suppose that teen 'chemistry' of yours has you ready for some 'good-man' shopping."

"Sure." I wasn't sure. My head was still awhirl after Father's speech. It was all so unexpected. I turned the ring between my fingers. The diamond wasn't very big.

"In case you are worried about your father entering politics—do not. He is a better man than you know."

"Oh, I know," I said with clever sarcasm.

"Do not be angry with me. I humor him, hoping he will meet new people, to prod him out of his bereavement."

"What if they martyr him, first?"

"You have to be a threat to earn a murder."

"What about the wolf who comes to us in wolf's clothing? Colonel Sohrabi."

"Dr. Delkash is no threat to Sohrabi. The good doctor will attend a few rallies, get distracted, and live happily ever after. You should join him, now that girls can vote at sixteen. You will meet a new group—a socially aware group."

"No political rallies for me," I said with a light-hearted lift of my chin.

Uncle Solomon's finger shook stridently in the air. "It is your civic duty."

"And shout political chants? Not me. That's how chants become headline clichés . . . something a fool quotes as fact. The larger the group, the more prone it is to manifestos and marching songs."

"Since the Revolution, girls vote." Uncle Solomon turned his head. "A girl your age needs politics and politics needs you."

I'm not sure if Uncle Solomon sees it. Father isn't courageous, the way Dr. Mousa was. Father is the gentle sort. A man with a big heart. No bigger sucker than a naïve man. A timid man opens his family to victimization by brazen scoundrels who aren't naïve, in the least.

Uncle Solomon must know Father has no natural protection against devious men. Quick to concede in every dispute. Father never speaks with bitterness, no matter how awful the subject. If there are such people—people without rancor—Father would be their icon. I've never heard him revile a false friend, shame a hypochondriac, nor speak ill of a bothersome neighbor. Yet, he could charm a fat kid off an aashpazi.

Because, he's earnest.

People love earnest. He stands straight. Not a man at cross purpose with the universe. He speaks whatever words need to be said. He's got a face that conniving politicians want to paste across their scheme-of-the-month, a pleasant face to hide a faulty construct. But, when the tide turns, that's the very face opposition hangs in Azadi Square!

Earnest, but he's no leader. He's too busy finding the center of every debate, the better angel in every opponent, the way to end every conflict with a kind word.

Wait a minute . . . he'll probably sit on the council that sends Armand to the frontline. What a dope. I can't imagine a man more ill prepared for politics. I lunged forward and grabbed Uncle Solomon's shoulder. "No good can come from this, not for anyone."

"This world is too cruel to be alone in," Uncle Solomon said, "and your father needs to jump in with both feet. Maybe I am forcing the athletic metaphor, but he deserves better than this sad life of a widower."

"Speaking of athletics, how did you know so much about Bosco's background? You couldn't learn all that from riding bikes together."

This time Uncle Solomon wasn't so quick with his words. "He told me."

"You can talk to monkeys?"

"Well, he showed me. The other details I picked up from the Imams."

"Are you two close? Because he hates me."

"No, that cannot be. I will not accept it. I will take you to meet him, for a formal introduction. Think of that: the three of us—friends."

*   *   *

I followed Uncle Solomon down the Monkey Bar's back alley. We found Bosco sitting on the edge of a Coca-Cola pallet with his head buried in his hands. I've never seen a monkey constantly in the throes of despair. Such a dark thinker.

I caught a glimmer of something around his neck, a Star of David, embedded with diamonds. He occasionally sniffed at it. I suspected it had been placed on him as some sort of a slur—an expensive insult by any measure. A monkey, wearing a Star of David. That's not normal.

Iran simmers with hard-boiled non sequiturs. We have more Jewish synagogues than any other Islamic nation, but our Jews respect Islamic law. They don't go around wearing a blasphemy. Jewish law and Islamic law both prohibit idolatrous symbols around our necks. Jewish law and Islamic law have nearly identical dietary restrictions. We hate each other . . . until dinner time.

Islam allows Bosco to race bicycles, but not me. More than anything, I would love to ride a bike some cool evening—the way Uncle Solomon does. I imagine it would be the next-best thing to flying. Such freedom. I can't even imagine that much freedom.

"Wait here," Uncle Solomon pushed me back while he approached Bosco.

They greeted one another, but on very somber terms. That worried me. What if Bosco didn't want to know me? And Bosco kept shaking his head . . . a lot. Uncle Solomon walked away, groaning, head down.

"What's wrong?" I asked.

"He's not one to make new friends. Unsociable." Uncle Solomon put his arm over my shoulder, but instead of leading me away, he led me toward Bosco. "But, he's curious. The diamond in your pocket . . . he can smell it."

I searched Uncle Solomon's eyes, puzzled. "No one can smell diamonds."

"This one can. Just you watch. When he sees me with my arm around you, he will consider that a marital bond. He reveres marital bonds . . . and diamonds."

There I stood, in front of the most unpleasant monkey in Iran. I'd been through that before and he nearly set me aflame. He jumped down and wrapped his arms around me—tight. All three of us stood in the dirty back alley of the Monkey Bar, hugging. It sounds gross, but I bawled and wiped tears away for the rest of the day.

I can't explain it. I looked in his eyes and something was looking back. Connection is a powerful thing.

Eleven

The second my eyes closed, I was with the dead. In a jumbled, fragmented moment of consciousness, I barely sensed the nightmare that churned about me, but was keenly aware of my soul's desperation to be awakened.

Blame love for your most beautiful dreams and your ugliest nightmares. Doctors used to call cancer *self-consumption*. Love has been that way for me— gnawing at my heart while I slept. I dream because that's what life is—fragments of this and that.

As the night advanced, I struggled and wept, sinking deeper into the jaws of love's cannibalistic nightmare. Yet, the approaching nightmare never lessened. I watched Armand as he ran from Iraqi shock troops, cringing, dodging bombs and bullets. He ran toward an ephemeral, ghostly, Eiffel Tower, a sparkling haven that beckoned in the distance. But no matter how fast he ran, it never got closer. I yelled, *Don't give up!*

I don't think he heard me.

Awakened by the Devil himself, I sat up. My head smoldered like a spent match as the last vestiges of my dream dissipated. The worst nightmares are those not too far from truth. Dizzy, I rubbed my eyes, still blurred with horrible images. I sat there, panting, between nightmare and noon, incapable of leaving my bed.

I knew it was silly to blame a pillow, nonetheless, I threw mine across the room . . . and cursed it. I'll never lay my head on that haunted thing again. When a Jinn inhabits something, who could say whether it whirled into my ear, into my mind, and twisted otherwise pretty dreams, thus making mental movies where it staged sadistic scenes about loved ones? The thought gave me such shivers that I staggered from bed and threw on my robe, anxious to leave a room still thick with premonitions.

Auntie Esther was already waiting for me at the bottom of the spiral staircase. She always had a tea towel draped over one arm. A stiff-figured Egyptian woman, stout, with strands falling from an impromptu bun, poorly constructed atop her head. Black hair with white streaks, like milk in tea before it's stirred. None of us wore headscarves inside the compound, so hair was its own message. Esther's hair said *experience.*

Combine experience with constant suspicion and you get a detective. I'll have to warn Zoe that Esther sees all. It's no use to plan mischief, since Esther can read minds. I'm not sure why I smile when she's in the room. Maybe she comforts me, the way some common annoyance feels like home; an old familiar gate that needs oiling; exterior walls painted the wrong color, easy to spot from miles away. That was our dear Auntie Esther, always going about the house with a tired, pained expression. She's bothersome in most ways, but she's ours, a reliable fixture in the Delkash compound.

I must have looked a mess. I certainly felt it.

Unsympathetic as ever, she pushed an envelope in my face. "Note, delivered this morning." She made it sound like bad news, or that I had done something wrong. It wasn't a standard-sized envelope, more like an invitation. This had never happened before. An envelope with my name, written in beautiful Farsi script.

The mere anticipation of reading someone's gracious words lifted me two feet off the ground. Some prominent person—probably Armand's parents—came all this way with an engraved invitation. *Aha*, Armand must have insisted.

The library.

They were probably in the library awaiting my answer. I quickly pulled the hood of my robe over my hair. I slid open the library's oak doors, wearing my best expression of surprise . . . but no one was there. I ran to our entry and looked out into the courtyard.

Empty.

In an odd mix of relief and disappointment I returned to Esther. "Where are they?"

Esther's classic hand-on-hip pose telegraphed her message long before she spoke. "If I don't know person, I don't let through gate. Doctor's five-step security program."

"What did they look like?" I asked.

"Not *they*. Just Russian lady. Passed note through face plate. Blonde hair and ugly accent."

More perplexed than ever, I broke the wax seal on the envelope and fished out a scented square of paper, bright and lemony. I looked for the sender's name.

Ava Herat?

She must have paid a hostess from the Monkey Bar to deliver it.

Esther shook a scolding finger at me. "Doctor don't want vanilla Asians in house. Tell her, don't come back."

"Esther! Chekov was Russian; Nabokov was Russian. What Father *doesn't* want in his house is prejudice."

Esther pushed me aside, yanked the tea towel from her arm and pout-scrubbed the counter tops.

I took a seat at our dining room table to read my fragrant invitation. Eventually, Esther pushed a hot plate of breakfast *rumbling* across the table—ceramic on wood.

Everyone else in the house, the early risers, had already finished their breakfasts. She didn't say it, but I would bet diamonds she weighed whether or not to feed me. I had, after all, chastised her, accused her of bigotry.

"What note say?" she snapped.

"It's an invitation for tea at—" The note said the *Monkey Bar balcony*, but I dared not utter those words aloud. I had never been up to the balcony. Muscle-bound guards stood behind velvet ropes and decided who could and couldn't pass.

Ava had the kind of social life that required a calendar, bracketed by the hour. She gave me an afternoon slot. It concluded with a hilarity: *bring Sarah and Zoe.* "It's an invitation for tea. I'll decline, of course. Your breakfast is plenty for me."

Finally, Auntie Esther smiled. "More like lunch," she added with a bit of lecture in her tone. She was proud of her breakfasts—even at this hour. Again, the countertops got another polishing, this time with love and self-satisfaction.

*   *   *

"Come in, it's not locked."

"Good afternoon. It's me and Sarah."

Big surprise. Like it could be anyone else. Let me run through all the options: Zoe and Sarah, or, Sarah and Zoe. Auntie Esther never came upstairs and Father has never set foot in my room. "Are you coming in or not?"

Always one for dramatics, Zoe opened my bedroom door, slow as a curtain call. Not far behind, Sarah nudged her forward. Zoe spun inside, twirling in ballerina circles, showing off her costume: leg lacings, tutu, leotard, tiara, slinging her long black silky hair as she turned.

"Sarah," I complained, "why didn't you invite me? Maybe I wanted to dress-up Zoe." I'm not one to complain, but it seemed to me Sarah dressed Zoe fifty-two percent of the time.

Before a word left Sarah's mouth, her face transmitted its cautionary scowl. "Zoe heard about the monkey races and wants you to take her to the Monkey Bar."

"Ha!" I slapped my hand over my mouth. It was never my intent to be rude or excluding. Too late.

Zoe's smile melted away. "What's so funny about that? I want to see the monkeys."

Unknown to her, she *had* been invited. I still held Ava's invitation in my hand, but I hid it behind me. "And so you shall, when you're old enough."

Zoe folded her arms. "You're only a year older than I am."

"But I look twenty-one." I felt judgment in the air. Sure enough, I looked behind Zoe, just in time to see Sarah roll her eyes. Sarah failed to realize I had grown up, transformed by love. And I looked every day of twenty-one.

No matter.

Zoe's hurt feelings were my main concern. "A youthful appearance is always better . . . in the long run. Stay away from the Monkey Bar. That place is filled with rude boys. Think of the advantages: you won't have to drive away their unwanted attention. I mean, really. You haven't noticed, but sometimes I come home frazzled. Exhausted."

"I wouldn't mind," said Zoe. "I like boys." She tried to conceal her smile with compressed lips. Yet, a ghost of hope still flickered in her pale, tea-colored eyes.

"Boys!" I scolded. Since Zoe faced me, she couldn't see Sarah's face fill with horror, but my expression was on full display. "Well, don't let them know that! That's a fool's trip down heart-break lane."

Truth?

Sarah and Zoe will never experience heart-break. Not with Zoe's silky black hair and graceful limbs, or Sarah's angelic face and soft curves. Mother's beauty and my cleithrophobia are two opposite sides of a very cruel coin. On her side, beauty. Without god-given beauty, an ordinary girl like me is always on the outside, locked, blocked, or limited. Beautiful women float through life's barriers at will.

I crumpled Ava's invitation, still hidden behind me. The last thing I needed was Sarah and Zoe intruding on my world—my very small world. They would have their Armands, whereas my Armand was slipping through my fingers.

I don't see me in his eyes anymore.

I've petitioned every twinkling star in the sky until they've wearied of my voice, and I'm nowhere near finished with my pleadings. My broken heart was spilling everywhere, and my new friends at the Monkey Bar had started to notice.

There is so much of life that Zoe will taste and relish. And it drives me crazy. In my outings, I've felt every wall, every obstacle, every lock holding me back.

My lack of beauty . . . it hurt, and deprived me of Armand's full attention.

Twelve

A lot goes through my mind while standing in the Monkey Bar's dark, dark, entrance hall. I smooth out the wrinkles in Ava's invitation while passing time. Tea on the balcony is a new pinnacle in my uneventful life. I wonder if others will join us. I wonder if tea is some elaborate matchmaking scheme and Ava is about to introduce me to Armand's parents. Won't she be surprised to find out they are old family friends.

Not too far away, I hear Armand's voice. I place my hand over my heart to hide its *thumping*. I lean in his direction. I can't hear everything, but enough to know he's the prominent voice at his table. Others listen, too timid to interrupt.

I can just imagine the headlines in Paris: Girl Marries Into Diplomatic Dynasty! I'm sure Father will eventually stumble across an article in the *Tehran Times*. Then he'll remember my hints, and all the pieces will fit. He'll have a big laugh and all will be normal again. All this might take weeks. I'll probably have to place limits on local journalists. *No interviews today*, I'll tell them. Because, I've heard paparazzi can undermine a couple's romantic life.

That won't do.

I shouldn't agitate over the future.

A lot can go through a girl's mind while she stands in the dark, waiting in the entrance hall.

After my eyes adjust, I see everyone at Armand's table. They watch him in rapt attention, their brows arching in awe at his lionhearted stories, leaning forward, eyes dancing in admiration. His table is always a place of magic. Let his friends have their moment. My visit has an entirely different purpose, but every bit as intoxicating: Armand's heart.

I hope Armand looks up to see me, and realizes how interesting I am—dining on the balcony—invited.

I don't know how to describe it, but the more I stare at him, the more it all adds up. I still see him as the boy who sat with me at Park-e Jamshidieh, in Tehran. He made jokes, calling it Park-e Jamileh. He bought a box of crusted saffron rice cakes from a pushcart. His mother yelled at him and made him share with me.

The point is, he did.

He complained bitterly to his mother that our family had no boys, but our mothers were college friends, from the same small town. Hamadan. Those were the days when our families vacationed together, until his father's assignment to France. I suspected, even back then, we were meant for each other, because our mothers had so much in common.

I stay in the entry and re-read Ava's invitation. I dare not tell her that my smile belongs to Armand. She would likely have some hurtful thing to say. Maybe she would try to drive a wedge between us.

Oh, how my heart aches. Armand is my first thought in the morning, my final thought at night.

I linger in the Monkey Bar's entrance, wishing, hoping I will overhear him speak my name. Maybe I will hear him tell his friends a childhood story about me . . . with a sigh.

A sudden round of applause startles me. The great champion Bosco, crossing the finish line, no doubt. How the roar of desperate gamblers disgusts me. So covetous. My heart sours at Armand's humiliation. I don't like watching such a well-bred boy demean himself with vices common to working men.

I've heard a man will change his life if the right woman comes along. I'm desperate to convince him: It's me. I'm that woman!

I cough, suddenly nauseated from the thick air that comes with any gathering of men. Just as well. I'm imagining too much, thinking too much, presuming too much.

I hear a familiar voice from the opposite side of the room—a discordant voice. Begging Giti's voice? Through a haze of hookah-pipe smoke, I spot her in the ladies' section, far from the race track. That doesn't add up. She has no money for dining out. She must be someone's charity. I decide to make my way over, before going upstairs.

An ear-piercing screech fills the air. Despite my prior warnings, Giti had hugged her monkey waiter. I arrive as the hostess takes the little monkey in her arms.

"Don't vurry," says the Russian hostess, "he no bite. Pulled teeth."

Pulled teeth! No wonder Bosco never smiles. That's so dictator!

What a fitting metaphor: Iran's politicians disarm innocent citizens the same way. Which dungeon had the Basij put our toothless smiles in?

The hostess wears a face of stone, watching us through unrelenting intelligent eyes. She reads the shock on my face and shrugs. "Vat? Da monkeys love it. No more bite in cages."

Oblivious to the hostess, Giti beckons me with a flurry of little waves. "Jamileh, I want you to meet Bahar, a tour guide from St. Thaddeus. I'm showing her our local sites. Sit, join us."

I nod and thank Bahar for her hospitality.

Bahar, however, doesn't respond with much enthusiasm. To the contrary, she looks drained and resentful. No doubt Giti had shaken her down for everything she was worth. Giti is a sly one, knowing whose pot to spoon from.

As I lean toward Giti, I telegraph with subversive eye flare. "Iran forbids women to attend soccer events, but they never complain when we spend our money here, at the monkey races."

"Don't be such an emotional hemophiliac," Giti says. "We only have one option. Where is the dilemma in that? That's the difference between you and me. I accept my one option. Deal with it."

Reset.

I take a cleansing breath while looking around the room. Thursday has a bonus race: Little-Monkey Marathon. They ride dogs, instead of bicycles. Whiplash is the odds-on favorite. He is quite a determined racer . . . for a young squirrel monkey. Mounted atop a Scottish Collie, Whiplash always electrifies the crowd with his uncanny ability to hang on. He's one of the most popular draws on the Gypsy rodeo circuit that tours our great nation.

Next, came the lowest-ranking bicycle racers. Their inability is part of the fun, but today, they were crazier than usual. Between their wobbling and lack of concentration, three have reversed course, heading in the wrong direction. The funniest part is watching their faces as the frontrunners speed directly at them.

I pull anxiously at my bottom lip, anticipating broken monkey bones. "Uh-oh!"

But, the referees are quick to grab the wayward racers and pull them off the track, just as the frontrunners whiz by. After the lead monkeys pass, the refs return the contrary amateurs to the track and give them a push-off in the proper direction. Soon they're back in the race, flashing the biggest monkey grins I've ever seen—toothless monkey grins, of course.

"The premium racers are up next," says Giti. "Oh, look. Bosco is in the lineup. I'm sure he'll win."

"He always does." From the other side of the room, Bosco looks directly at me and gives me a subdued wave.

"I think Bosco is waving at you," says Giti.

I nod. "We've made our peace." Bosco still frightens me, but I want Giti to think I have a way with monkeys.

"I wish he'd wave at me," she says. "I like monkeys. They try so hard."

I look around for Armand. Still sitting at his table, he shakes a fist full of money and takes bets on the second-place contender. That's where the big money is. No one ever bets on first place, because Bosco always takes first place.

I can't believe I know handicapping facts like that. It just goes to prove how bad association quietly corrupts us, before we realize it.

The Monkey Bar, tea on the balcony, Armand, bare-back dog races: What a beautiful afternoon. An air-conditioned building, full of laughter, far from the Basij, surrounded by friends I've known all my life (with the exception of the humorless Bahar). Our village is lucky to have such innocent distractions, as if the Caspian Sea isn't blessing enough.

"Giti," I say, "has Ava approached you about work?"

"No."

"My goodness, Giti, you're a buffet of bad news, from appetizer to dessert." No job offer means no future and she's only weeks away from eviction at the orphanage. Then again, I may need someone to lighten my duties in Paris. As long as she uses her opportunistic talons in my service, she might even contribute toward expenses. "Giti, have you ever considered working outside of Iran?"

"If I had the money to travel, sure."

"Have you ever considered Paris?"

"I would rather go to Western America."

She's just seventeen. Giti thinks living in Hollywood will launch her life into happily-ever-after.

Hardly.

She doesn't realize America will pull her deeper into the jaws of godlessness. Madonna is American. Enough said. "Would you consider going to Paris, with me?"

Giti rocks back and forth in her chair, straining in thought. "Oh, I think we should choose America. Let's go to America."

I've never heard her speak so implausibly. What does she know about America? "Their imperialism scares me. They have electrical wires in every wall. I'm sure that affects the cerebral cortex. And, they have crocodiles . . . or alligators. I'm not sure I could distinguish one from the other."

Without so much as a smile, Giti swallows before answering. "One will see you later, the other, will see you in a while."

I'm certainly no expert on America, but I've never heard anything so foolish. "I don't see your point."

Giti shrugs. "I haven't worked out all the language details, but the method of interpretation can be found in Western music." She grips the edge of her chair and leans forward. "The Sufis say: 'We gain wisdom a step at a time.'" She sighs in exasperation. "I will listen more carefully next time."

A hand seizes my shoulder. In a startle, I turn.

A tall Russian hostess stares down at me. No smile. "Come," she says curtly.

Half scared, half excited, I follow. I'd never been upstairs. Upstairs is where the North Koreans spend their afternoons, segregating themselves, far above regular customers. I knew about the security guards at the bottom of the stairs, but not at the top. Upstairs, the guards are bigger, shirtless, blond and blue-eyed. They glare at us with folded arms. Imposing men, with Uzis strapped across their backs.

Both step aside for the Russian hostess. Despite the Uzis, I doubt they were Jews, more like blue-eyed Jinns. Amr ibn Juwain, the venerable Arab poet, said *I warned Ibn Ammar, and told him, do not trust the man who has blue eyes and blue hair.* Enough said.

The Koreans had lechery in their eyes. The women attending them were shamelessly compliant and immodest. My face turns hot and prickly, my heart moans *Cancel your invitation!* The furnishings up here are much more luxurious, but unlike downstairs, women sit at the same table as men. And . . . they're touching, in public.

Is this the direction I want my life to go? I've often asked myself, what can a good woman do until the Mahdi comes? Whether I serve in a mosque, in a household, or in the Department of Agriculture, a woman's hands can do good, even where a man's can't. In these last few months, I had just begun to see the possibilities. I wanted clean hands, hands that could support a diplomat's aspirations, raise his children, be their inspiration. If I manipulate, seduce, and trick my way through life, I'll contaminate my feminine gifts. The people most important to me will always feel the difference.

This is not a place I want to be. I turn to leave, but the Russian hostess grabs my arm with a grip as powerful as a man's. As I think about it, she bears a strong resemblance to a man. A hardened spirit flickers behind her pale-blue eyes until they burn like lasers. "Walk," she says in her gruff, hateful voice.

Thirteen

"Get your Marxist hands off me—you—vanilla Asian!" I slung loose and jerked away from the hostess. I adjusted my headscarf, never breaking eye contact with this foreign table servant. Guests on the balcony stopped what they were doing and sneered their disapproval.

In that instant, I was filled with shame, having realized some people are blatantly narrow minded. And, by *people,* I meant, me. I sounded as racist as Auntie Esther. May Allah overlook my *faux pas*. On the other hand, the hostess didn't seem perturbed—in the least. Probably didn't understand a word of Farsi.

Wasted prayer.

I spotted Ava at a table near the balcony's railing. She stood and marched stiff legged straight toward me. I had a weird feeling she was about to hit me, given her rate of speed, and clenched fists.

"You did *not* bring your zisters."

I assumed a slight crouch, ready to duck at her first swing. "Tutors. They scheduled poor Sarah and Zoe months ago. Their schedules are crammed with homework, essays, and piano lessons. Sarah begged me to ask your forgiveness."

Truth? Sarah would rather stick needles in her eyes than set foot in the Monkey Bar.

Ava's eyes searched my face for thanklessness.

But I stared straight back, expressionless as a plate.

"Very well, take a seat." Ava gestured toward her ring-side, sky-high table. Still standing, she brushed and smoothed the folds of her outfit.

As usual, she was a veritable golden platter of fashion. She wore an Arwa Al-Banawi. Everything Arwa produced was contemporary, infused with Bedouin references. Another step forward in female empowerment. "Does dis jilbab make my shoulders look wide?"

I paused, somewhat flattered. "Are you actually asking for my opinion?"

"I know," Ava said in mock exaggeration. "What is wrong wit me?" She took the chair across from me. Between us, a large manila envelope with Sarah's name on it. "I have bad news."

I loved Ava's French accent, but with it, she often tortured me. Giti said, she's an iceberg waiting for a *Titanic*. When I told Giti that Ava was twenty-one, Giti got angry with me. *She's about as twenty-one as the Whore of Babylon. More like thirty.* I'm not one to let poor people shape my thoughts, but there was some truth in Giti's observations.

Meanwhile, the tea boy rolled his cart to our table. It was neatly set with geometric selections of cute single-servings: baked goods and a small international display of tea bags. I knew what I wanted: Persian rose-petal tea. But, never-to-be-satisfied Ava hesitated, studying the cart with concentration normally reserved for chess.

"Too late in da day for tea. Bring water pipe wit Moroccan hash." With a weary swipe of her hand, she dismissed the tea maker. She turned to me, much the afterthought, and motioned for him to return. "And you?" she opened her palm, offering any and everything on the cart.

The tea boy paused and leaned forward to prompt my order.

"Just rose-petal tea for me. Hashish damages motor control—neuropathy."

"Ha!" chortled Ava. "*Chiant*. I once read about da pitfalls of hashish . . . I simply put da book down." She raised her hands above the table as though washing them. "And dat was dat."

I usually got most of what Ava said, but sometimes she used French slang and all I could do was respond to the words I understood.

Service was a lovely ritual. With one fluid motion, the tea boy smiled, bowed, placed rose-petal tea and adorable little fig tarts in front of me, then, he stood straight as a column and pushed his cart away. I could see why big spenders preferred the balcony.

I'd never seen such a tea cart. It was a marvel of craftsmanship: metal tubes, soldered and chromed to match the same hue as the oversized silver teapot on top. I enjoyed watching Ava's reflection as it rolled away.

Ava was accustomed to getting whatever she wanted, but I was never certain what she wanted. I hoped the tea boy knew the difference. I could just imagine him going downstairs, into the alley, and paying some shady character to fill Ava's hashish order—assuming she was serious.

Her lips turned in a grim slant. "Now, back to my bad news. Armand was officially inducted into da military."

I gasped. "I just saw him downstairs."

"He does not know."

We stared at each other across the table, without so much as a blink, both knowing what his induction meant. There was a fine line between duty and suicide. But, if Armand survived, he would return a hero . . . with his pick of women. He would be paraded through Noshahr, beyond my reach. My Armand hopes, my Armand yearnings . . . my Armand mirage.

"Do you not want da good news?"

"Good news for Iran or me?"

"For you."

Well, that was unexpected. "By all means, what's *my* good news?"

Ava leaned forward, one eyebrow raised. "I could be persuaded to purchase airfare to Paris for Armand, you, and your zisters. Dat's why I asked you to bring your zisters. I need der agreement." She leaned back, kissed the tips of her fingers, and tossed them heavenward. "Da Eiffel Tower iz a monument to romance, beautiful lacings of steel. Kiss Armand in its lacy shadow. Study Western books. Come back wit your Western degrees. By dat time, Iran would have seen two regime changes. Iran has short memory. All your offences will have been forgotten."

I wanted to leap from my chair, climb the velvet drapes and proclaim Armand's deliverance. But I held my tongue. "I wasn't called to war. Why tell me?"

Ava looked to her left, then to her right. "So many elephants in da room." She threw her head back with a high-pitched cackle. "I do not know, maybe da way your heart melts every time he enters da room; maybe da way you stalk him in da marketplace?"

"I do not!"

"I have watched tru my windowpane. Really, Jamileh, you are shameless."

"Your windowpane? Where do you live?"

With a lazy spin of her finger, she pointed straight up. "Upstairs . . . up upstairs."

I looked up at the ceiling. "In the Monkey Bar?"

"I own da *une boite*, how you say— dis establishment. Da tird story is a penthouse—my penthouse. Overlooks da marketplace. Do not let dat get around. We bot have secrets."

I had underestimated Ava. What a clever woman she must be—to own such a successful enterprise in a man's world. This new piece of the puzzle was like a splash of hot tea in my face, bringing me a new clear-headed respect for Ava. Money motivated, crass, non-religious, a human pun, but Ava was anything but witless. And she wanted me to share her secret. What was that about?

Was she a spy? A double agent? Ava probably hadn't been Ava in years. Even her name might be made-up, a smokescreen. Ava probably laughs at us Persians. Persian and Parisian: so similar in pronunciation, so different in ideology. She probably amuses herself watching our failed regime changes; probably mocks the very laws that she subverts to

create new streams of revenue. In a sea of Islamic
zealots aching for entertainment, she has devised a
thousand ways into our pockets through free
enterprise.

Who was Ava—really? She must be a practitioner
of obfuscations, full of left-turns and surprises, a
human riddle. Yet, Ava was the only one who looked
after me . . . or Armand, for that matter.

I reached across the table to examine the envelope
with Sarah's name on it.

Fast as a snap, Ava yanked it out of my reach.
"So, are you and Armand ready for Paris?"

No longer confident of my secrets, I hedged. "I'm
still not clear on how I fit in."

"However you want. My only condition is dat you
and your zisters go. If dey agree, I will provide airfare
from Azerbaijan to Paris."

"It's cheaper if we depart from Tehran. I've
priced it."

"Do you have passport?" she asked with a head-
wagging smirk. "You would be pulled from da plane
in handcuffs. Leaving requires more dan a plane ticket.
Dis midnight escapade requires money, fake
documents, and foreign connections."

"But I doubt if Sarah would go. If Sarah refuses,
Zoe would certainly refuse."

"Do you want to save Armand or not?"
Suddenly, my dreams were coming to life. Ava had
brought the once ephemeral, ghostly, Eiffel Tower
nearly within grasp. "Yes, but it seems so peccant."

"Peccant?" Ava folded her arms, amused. She seemed to enjoy the taste of the word. "Peccant."

"It means—"

She raised her hand, stopping me in mid-sentence. "I know what it means. But dis is da first time I've heard it used in common conversation. Where did you get such a vocabulary?"

"Reading. What else do I have to fill my days?"

Ava reached out and took my hand. "Go shopping. Buy small suitcase . . . for Paris."

*   *   *

Despite Ava's strange ways, I descended the stairs with more wanderlust than when I ascended. She had filled my head with extraordinary thoughts, regaling me with stories about French girls. They wear boy boxer shorts to bed, with boy tee-shirts. The idea intrigued me.

As I descended the wide carpeted steps, I caught a glimpse of Giti ducking out the back door. Yet, humorless Bahar was still seated at their table. Bahar was exchanging notes—probably telephone numbers—with Armand's best friend, Amjad Never-Had-A-Job Kalif. *Good luck with that, Bahar.*

Why was Giti in such a rush?

I made my way toward the back door, through the smoke, the hubbub of gamblers, and bottle-carrying monkeys. When I opened the service door, Giti's head hung over a litterbin. Except for Giti, the alley was calm—not a sound. The silence accentuated her woeful moans, heaving, retching, and crying.

Gently, I put my hand on her back to reassure her. "I'm here, Giti. I'm here." She has a nervous stomach, prone to spasms when emotional.

She turned, and to my wonder, lunged at me with fury in her eyes. "Do you know what they're doing in there? They're throwing away more money in ten minutes than our orphanage spends in a month. Do you want to know what's wrong with Iran? Open that door. Have a look. Decadence. Hedonism."

I adjusted her crooked scarf and let my hand run down the side of her face. "They're just young men. They don't understand."

Giti covered her face with both hands and burst into tears. "I know—unsympathetic young men. I couldn't stand another minute of that. I'll never set foot in that place again."

Above us, an ember glowed bright through the darkness. Startled, I moved away, my back against the brick wall. Giti stumbled off in the opposite direction.

But, there was no danger. It was Bosco, watching us, with his legs crossed, cigarette between two fingers, eyes lit with amusement.

"Does he bite?" Giti asked.

I nearly laughed. "They pulled his teeth. Remember? And you think your life is rough?" I know it's rude to point, but I had no other option. "Imagine his."

"Can I hug him?" Giti whispered.

"I don't know. We've become friendly, but I've never tested those boundaries." I spread my arms. "Hello Bosco."

He threw his cigarette aside and climbed down from the empty Coca-Cola crates. He waddled over and gave me a big hug. Giti joined us—group-hug style. Suddenly, the alley didn't seem so dirty. I'm sure monkey hairs were getting on my abaya. Even that didn't bother me. Everything seemed right, as it should be. Three sad monkeys consoling one another.

Our fates were sealed, at the same moment, in the same alley. Giti was the first to stop hugging. She had a lost gaze as she stepped away from us, pacing in small circles, each pass gave her a broader smile.

Bosco pointed to something in the sky.

Giti paused to follow Bosco's sight line, high in the sky, looking straight toward a shooting star. We all watched as it melted into the horizon.

Giti pulled off her headscarf and shook her hair free. Her long wavy hair glistened in the moonlight. She sighed at the lush sweep of stars above us. "Remember when I was ten? We used to meet at the shoreline. Your mother brought chicken and sweet tea."

"We still can," I said.

"Your mother is dead. The difference between me and you? I no longer follow my heart. Yesterday is gone. Our mothers are gone. We were so foolish then . . . thinking the world was ours to conquer, almost within reach. Did our childhood really happen? Did I just imagine all that? How did we get to this?"

Giti was right about *her* dismal life, but she was nothing like me. My heart still sparkled with love. "When you love someone—as a kid—it never leaves. That's the shy love that never dies, darting from one heart chamber to the next. Father once explained circulation in those terms. He said our blood runs frantically searching one chamber and then the other, hoping to find the first spark that made our life. Falling in love is like that."

"Sounds beautiful . . . really," Giti said. "I wish it were true, but what I saw inside— I had always imagined—hoped—that if others knew how orphans lived, they would climb over one another to rescue us. Now I know what runs through the chambers of their hearts. They don't care." Her tears returned.

The back door opened and out stepped Ava. Her eyes widened, surprised to see Giti. "Aw, my tearful little vagrant, what is da matter? Is it dat bad haircut?"

Giti quickly tied her scarf on.

"If you intend to survive dis jihadist nightmare, you must do a lot of smiling on da outside while crying on da inside." She turned to me with a sly smile. "It is far easier to deny a first love for da joy of da many dat follow."

"That's not very lady like," Giti said, in what little voice she had left.

"Neither is your mustache," Ava enunciated, syllable by syllable. Ava raised her fist, but, instead of striking Giti, she stomped away, on grimy cobblestones, toward a long dark vehicle waiting at the end of the alley. The back door of the limo opened and in she went.

Money changed hands no doubt, but nothing that would find its way to the orphanage.

Giti looked down at Bosco. "Salty. I've seen some witches in my short life, but I'll need therapy to get over that lady-business."

Bosco stared back, lightly touching Giti's arm, but he said nothing.

Of course, there was no therapy in Giti's future. That was part of her humor. Orphans don't gamble or play golf . . . or get therapy.

Despite claims otherwise, money loves money, power chases power. Seems every society has an incestuous love fest of success marrying success. I noticed that much in private school. Far from poor people, the wealthy create a ruling class—intentional or not.

Seems the well-to-do can bend those in power to their will. The world is stacked against Giti, and people like her. Worse yet, Giti thought those in power wanted to rescue her.

I'm so tired of do-gooders and so-called philanthropists. Charitable organizations—religious and political—have an uncanny ability to grow a new layer with every passing year. Al-Haramain Islamic Foundation once rented the entire Monkey Bar for a night of fundraising. Charities are quick to accept highly publicized awards, while in the real world, hungry orphans hug monkeys in dirty alleys.

With the rich, it seems no good deed is done away from the spotlight. No charity filters down to our orphans. Awards, back slapping, speeches, lofty verbosity carried on the winds of politics. These are not pleasant thoughts, but true, nonetheless.

I'm so tired of poor people.

Fourteen

Mr. Oskou lifted Mother's three-carat diamond ring to catch the morning light pouring through his shop's window. He set his loupe on the glass counter and shook his head. "You must leave the ring and necklace for a proper appraisal."

"I will do no such thing," I shot back. "Do I have *idiot* written on this Persian forehead?"

He stepped back, arms dangling listlessly. "And you think I keep sufficient funds on hand for items of this quality? I'll have to confer with a banker for a short-term loan."

"A banker?" I leaned over the counter, whispering in the voice of someone sharing a confidence. "How much did you intend to borrow?"

"Please," his voice sharp and firm, "some matters are still considered proprietary between a pawn broker and his banker. You know who I am. You know my family, and I know yours. I could not stay in business if I cheated the good doctor's favorite daughter."

I doubt he intended to hurt me, but knowing I was the least perfect daughter opened an old wound. "I'm not his favorite daughter, and I'm not here to pawn Mother's ring. I'm taking it with me to Paris. I came to establish its value."

He plopped my ring on the counter and raised his hands toward heaven. "This is a business establishment. I am not one of your girlfriends to pick through your jewelry box with." He tried to look away from the winking ring laying on the counter, but I watched his hand move closer until he was touching, fondling, rolling it in his palm. He sighed, diamond-addicted.

"Look, Jamileh, you are not alone here. We are all trapped, maybe in different parts of Jahannam, but nonetheless trapped." His face softened into a warm smile. "I am not against you, dear. If you just want an opinion, mine would be a professional one. I charge for such things."

"That's all I ever wanted. What's your price for an evaluation?" I placed my purse on his counter and pulled out my wallet, yanking out paper bills. "How much?"

Mr. Oskou tugged at his collar, never breaking eye contact with my money. "Two-hundred Tomans."

Only twenty American dollars? His low rates startled me. Nonetheless, I registered my disapproval with a *clucking* noise of dissent. I had already priced airline tickets and was now money aware.

His dialect was Qajar, and they had an excellent reputation for good taste, perhaps an appraiser to be reckoned with. If Mr. Oskou had a fault, it was that of ostentation and a craving of fine jewelry. So, I thumbed through my money and put two-hundred Tomans on his counter.

He snatched it up and gave me an answer before he finished counting. "One-million-seven-hundred-thousand French francs. Congratulations, that's enough to pay cash for a small apartment in Paris." He picked up his loupe to steal one final look. He *mmm'd* as he rotated the diamond in the light. "Top quality. Of

MICHAEL BENZEHABE   119   PERSIANALITY

course, you could not get that price in Iran, but Europe teems with gullible shoppers."

I had no idea. My newfound wealth left me lightheaded. Suddenly, the world felt more convenient, more generous, wide open and waiting. I was a polliwog wriggling from the tight confinement of a small egg cluster into the larger world. I had this odd mixture of gratitude toward Mother and a prickly disbelief of Mr. Oskou's evaluation. "And what about the necklace?"

He held out his hand. His fingers beckoned with obnoxious little *give-me's*. Grudgingly, I laid out another two hundred. "There you have it, *shopkeeper*."

"Not as much as the ring, but your mother had a discerning eye. The necklace would easily fetch another four-hundred-and-twenty-thousand French francs."

Tuition! Zoe and I had played dress up with this jewelry, unaware of its true value. No one ever explains these things to kids. I'd spent two weeks agonizing over airfare, carfare, warfare, and welfare. No human should have to endure such torture. I had the answer with me the whole time. I was set for life and never knew it.

I once overheard Armand tell the boys at his table, *When good Persians die, they come back to life in Paris*. I'm a good Persian. I want to live. Enlivened with my newfound wealth, my sense of mischief had been aroused. I could feel the chains of Ayatollah Khomeini dropping off my ankles, handcuffs slipping

off my wrists, gates creaking open. I was free—really
free.

By coincidence, or providence, the Muezzin
called for the Zuhr prayer from his minaret. A sign?
Surely, Allah was blessing my journey. "Mr. Oskou,
you barely gave the ring a glance. How can you be
sure?"

"Not so long ago, your father brought the rough
stone to me. I know who cut it, I know who designed
the mounting. This ring and I go way back."

Four-hundred Tomans without one drop of sweat.
I resented his easy earnings. He knew the value of my
jewelry before I walked in the door. This villain was
no friend. Our families had shared meals, his fat
daughter worshipped at the same mosque, and now he
was shaking me down with the same enthusiasm he
cheated strangers. My appraisal no longer looked like
the good deal I imagined.

"He bowed, touching the fingers of his right hand
to his lips, then to his forehead.

I snatched up Mother's gifts and left Oskou's
Jewelry Shop. A new earth rumbled beneath my feet.
Everything felt money-distorted, escape-shaky, and
freedom-wobbly.

I knew Uncle Solomon was parked around the
corner, but the thought of so much money created a
silly grin I couldn't wipe off my face. Uncle Solomon
never missed such details, and would know something
major was afoot.

I needed time to collect myself—a delay.

In times of trouble, I was always drawn to the Caspian. I walked slower than everyone else, almost catatonic, heading straight into the breeze that rolled off the sea.

My Gucci boots carried me, mindlessly, over a flagstoned walkway, past silk merchants, food stalls, and hawkers of all descriptions. I found myself at the edge of the business district and walked along the bulwark that overlooked the lapping waves of the dark, cold sea below. The fresh air was splendid—bracing.

A seagull hovered just above my head, breaking off from her northbound journey. I hoped her crossing included a visit to the organ grinder in Azerbaijan. She descended to bid me farewell with a *screech*.

"Fly on my feathered sister," I called out, half in prayer, half in jest. "Tell the dancing monkey I'm bringing him a gold coin. He can dance for me, before I board my plane to Paris."

I no longer needed Ava's airline tickets. I had my own funds. I may be short a few forged documents, but the docks bristled with shady purveyors of fraud, deception, and impersonation. Surely *they* had access to such travel papers.

Dodging authority was an old trope in our culture.

Iran is such an ancient land. More are below its soil than above it. Here, even thoughts are old. Smiles have layers of double-meanings, and simple words carry religious baggage. But in Paris, even the moonlight is new—or so I've heard.

My walk back to the car was a mental torrent of plannings and imaginings. Yet, I vaguely remembered Uncle Solomon waiting, door open. Somehow, we left without me exposing my secret. I did remember that he latched my seatbelt. Somewhere along the way my mind cleared after realizing Uncle Solomon had been pleasure driving—no destination in particular.

"Uncle Solomon, what would you do if, one day, you realized you were free?"

"I am free."

"I mean, free to be whoever you wanted, free to go wherever. Free."

"I am not following you. I am free to do all those things. What do you mean?"

"Oh, Uncle Solomon, when you talk like that it makes me feel like you haven't been listening."

Uncle Solomon's face of servitude returned—that annoying uniform of cool distance.

"All I'm trying to say is this: You're just a driver, yet you can participate in the International Olympics. You can go places; you can meet interesting people, and never come back if you choose."

He sat stiffer than usual. *Just a driver* had offended him. I saw it in his face the instant I said it. But I needed him to hear me out.

"My husband will decide if I can, or can't, ride a bike. I must work for the good of our family enterprise—for my husband's name. When my beauty becomes insufficient—and it will—his attention is bound to wander elsewhere. Then comes my emotional exile. I will do what all women do, tend to matters in the marketplace, tend house, tend children. But women know when the blossom of love has wilted."

A clenched jaw told me Uncle Solomon wasn't listening. I had gone too far. He was hurt. Suddenly, *my* problem didn't seem so large. I leaned forward and touched his shoulder. "Of course you're so much more than a driver . . . to us. You can forgive me, if you want to."

Uncle Solomon eyed me up in his rearview mirror and wagged his head scornfully. "Thank you. Where would I be without your permissions?"

"I didn't say you had to. I meant, if you wanted to, it would show a flexibility that Allah would likely reward. I just wanted you to know how empty my life would be without you, should my husband take me someplace far away." I said it as if I cared. "You being a man and all, you'll always be going where men go, doing what men do." I leaned forward with tightened lips. "You know . . . be free."

Uncle Solomon pulled over and parked.

When he turned to face me, he had a smile. "I never looked at it that way, and maybe you shouldn't either. Let me rattle off some of those great privileges you think we men have."

"No!" I sank into my seat, annoyed. "Can't we just talk about girl jail? I mean, that's what never gets discussed, how women get erased. If I marry, I'll have to take my husband's name. I'll lose mine. More must be written about this strange custom."

His eyes missed nothing. He let me finish my protest, but never veered an iota from his original point. "I went to the same schools you went to. We were both taught the Sahara was once full of lakes and rivers. Recently, archeologists discovered a grave in Gobero, containing a young mother and her two children. No husband. Apparently, he survived. A forensic team established the cause of death: drowning. A river must have changed course. But it was the other details I remember so vividly . . . the *way* she was buried.

"The children were dressed perfectly, lovingly posed, facing their mother, all their hands entwined. The mother—wife—wore polished stones, and held a tortoise shell brush in one hand. *Who choreographed this?* I wondered. The mother and children were covered with layers and layers of flower petals. Who picked all those flowers and removed all those petals?"

"The husband?" I guessed.

"That would be my guess," said Uncle Solomon. "What jumped out at me was the detail he put into his goodbye, the love behind his reluctant farewell. This primitive man, this dirt farmer, this savage hunter, loved them.

"You can describe men as selfish monsters if you want to, but that does not match my observations. What I have seen is selfless service. On our way home, count the soldiers with missing limbs. Day in and day out, I see men working without complaint, husbands sacrificing, fathers swallowing their pride at work and coming home with reassuring smiles. Have you ever asked yourself, *why?*"

"They have to."

"No, they do not have to. They want to."

"No, they have to. That's their job. Uncle Solomon, what would you say if you found out I had my own place in Paris?"

"That would be good."

"Do you think someone my age could own an apartment in Paris?"

"Legally, you are too young to execute a contract, but with a financial trust, I am sure such a thing is possible—in your case, likely. Your father owns an apartment in London. Sarah will live there while she works on her Ph.D."

That surprised me. "No one told me." What a day. The whole adult world operated on a system I knew nothing about. I had never felt so excluded. "I knew Sarah would eventually attend a foreign university, but I didn't know Father owned a flat in London."

Uncle Solomon's face pinched quizzically. "I thought you knew. You will probably live there too, eventually."

"Well, I don't want to live in London, and this is an entirely different matter." I was near bursting. I had to tell someone. "I just discovered the value of my inheritance from Mother. With her ring and necklace, I can afford my own apartment and tuition."

"Jamileh, you have more than that. So do I."

I stared in disbelief. "Mother left you an inheritance?"

"Of course. I have enough to do something, but not enough to do nothing."

"Why didn't anyone tell me? Are we rich?"

Uncle Solomon suppressed his laughter. "Rich is a relative word, but by international standards, most people would say we have enough. The best way to describe us: we are off to a good start."

"It doesn't seem like it." *No electric lights* was my first thought. Maybe this is how a poor man sees things. As an orphan, Uncle Solomon probably thought he was arriving at a palace, that first night he came home with Mother. But, why would we live inside primitive stone blocks if we were so wealthy?

Rich people are usually pressed by suitors seeking marriage alliances for upward mobility. The only invitation I've ever received was from a woman—to tea, at the Monkey Bar. "Does Father ever make introductions for you?"

"Yes. Sarah is not the only one suffering from your father's attempts at matchmaking."

"Have you met someone?"

"No."

"Do you want to meet someone?"

"I would prefer to make my own introductions. Your father means well, but I am not the person he thinks I am. Let me leave it at that."

"You're gay."

"No, I am not gay."

"Yes, you are."

"I am Jewish. Introducing me to Muslim girls could get my head cut off." He rubbed gently at his neck and I got the impression he was recalling some of

Father's unwanted introductions. "Thank you, but no Muslim girls for me, Dr. Delkash." He spoke sharply as though Father was in the car.

"Jewish? Then, you're like Zoe."

"Yes."

So, that was the distance between us. I never would have guessed. He seemed so normal. "You're a handsome man, Uncle Solomon. My friends have always spoken highly of you. I've never heard a negative word."

"And I think highly of them . . . most of them."

"When Zoe gets older, you two would make a beautiful couple—if you don't mind waiting."

"I would never marry anyone from our household. She is my new sister. Dr. Delkash is our new father."

"That's how you think of us?"

"Of course."

That picture ricocheted through my head, odd and surprising. "Jewish. Why didn't you tell me?"

"You never asked." His russet eyes languished. "In all these years, never once did you ask." He gave his head a shake, and just like that, his smile was back. "Your Father and Mother never had the honor of meeting my family. They did not know my origin— nor did it matter. They took me in. They were good to me. Raised me as their own. And I loved them."

"I wondered about that. You've distanced yourself, lately. I suppose your Jewishness is taking root."

"Sorry. Iran has so many controlling men— Jewish and Muslim. I wanted to be someone you could talk to, without fear of judgment. I didn't want to come off as bossy or manipulative."

That hadn't crossed my mind, nor did it sound like a valid excuse. It was bad manners, plain and simple.

In the distance, I saw a strange sight. I blinked and strained my eyes to make sense of it. "Look, Uncle Solomon, a monkey, all by himself, riding a bicycle in broad daylight."

"That is Bosco."

"You can tell that's Bosco, from this distance?"

"Who else could it be? He is on his way to the zoo. Very sad."

"How do you know where he's going?"

"I go with him, sometimes."

"What does he do?"

"He brings chicken to his wife and son."

"He has a son?"

Uncle Solomon nodded.

I sat at attention. "Let's go with him."

"Oh, no. It is very sad."

I shoved his shoulder in protest. "That's why I want to see it."

He took a deep breath and shook his head. "You would not like what you see. Bosco has feelings. I have seen it. He aches for his wife and son. Shin Bone taunts him by mistreating them in his presence. Bosco is my friend, but sometimes— Well, sometimes I cannot bear it. I have to leave."

I sat forward, grasping the front seat. "Do you cry?"

"Not always, but I have, on occasions."

"You cry over a monkey. Just say it."

He wouldn't answer. Minutes passed. So, I sat back. Uncle Solomon was a strange creature. You think you know someone, and then life fills their head with the strangest ideas. What a puzzle-of-a-man. "You're controlling me."

"I am doing no such thing."

"Then, take me!" My tone was haughtier than I had intended. Perhaps it needed to be.

Fifteen

"How could Uncle Solomon do such a thing?" I buried my face in my duvet and wept.

Sarah's steps hurried to my bedside. "What did he do?" Then she whispered in my ear. "Should I send Zoe out of the room?"

"No." My sobs so profound I wavered between emotional exhaustion and physical paralysis—the vapors, I've heard it called. From the other side of my bed, Zoe stroked my hair. She said nary a word, knowing Sarah had eviction on the tip of her tongue.

"Devious Uncle Solomon," Sarah hissed, in a tone reserved to shame. "The last person I would have suspected. Cold as a lizard and ambitious as Lucifer. Did he hurt you?"

"No. *Yes!*"

"What did he do?"

"Wait," I moaned. "Roll me over. I haven't the strength to turn myself." With Sarah's hands pulling, and Zoe, from the other side, pushing. Soon, I was on my back. The air became fresh, cool, breathable.

Sarah was soon in my face. "Where does it hurt?"

My hand, weak and flailing, fell upon my chest.

Immediately, I felt their hands go to work opening my robe, until my bare flesh chilled in the cool air.

Sarah did that thing, squinting her eyes when my answer wasn't quite there. "He touched your breasts?"

"No. In here," I said, as I pounded my chest. I sat up, furious. "In my heart!" I let myself fall back into my pillows. "The worst place for misery. I can never unsee that horror—ever. It will be trapped inside, forever, putrefying all the other happy feelings. Smiles die that way."

"Girl hormones," Zoe mumbled, as if I wasn't there.

My head snapped in Zoe's direction. "It's not girl hormones. It's tragedy of the worst sort. I don't want to speak of it. It's— it's too awful."

"But you must." Sarah added a raised brow, as older sisters often do. "If Uncle Solomon is to remain in this household, I demand an explanation."

"I don't see anything," Zoe said, tugging at my open robe "certainly nothing that looks twenty-one."

Sarah didn't get it. Sure, I blamed Uncle Solomon, but the ugly memory inside me was Bosco—a painful Bosconian experience that Uncle Solomon deliberately burned into my mind, forever. I fell back, listless, supine, staring at nothing but white—my white stuccoed ceiling. Soon, two heads, Sarah and Zoe, popped into the periphery of my white panorama, wearing expressions determined to know more.

"It was awful, and I saw the whole thing." Feeling oddly displayed, I realized I was bare breasted. My fingers moved quickly, finding buttons and buttonholes, re-fastening my robe. "If I am to tell this—out loud—then both of you need to brush my hair. But, don't look at me."

"You'll have to sit up," Zoe said.

"Sit? I can't, not in this condition. Rub my feet. Yes, that would be best. Rub my feet and look away while I tell you what happened."

Both were surprisingly quick to obey; I suspected this newfound obedience was based mostly on salacious curiosity. I almost wished them gone— except they made such a lovely audience for my tragedy.

Where to begin? I mentally scrolled through the day's events. "Uncle Solomon took me to the zoo. An act for which I may never forgive him. We followed Bosco there."

"The arse biter?" Sarah asked.

"He's innocent," I thundered. "Don't you see? That was Shin Bone's crime—and Armand's. Shin Bone annihilated Bosco's family, robbed his son of his start in life. And stop interrupting. I want this to flow out of me, without doubts, obstacles, or accusations. Maybe then my heart can be cleansed of this foul memory.

"Anyway, me and Uncle Solomon got out of the *Monstrosity* and trailed Bosco inside the zoo. Bosco brought a bag of chicken. He must have stolen it from a street vendor—or maybe he paid for it, but without pockets I'm not sure where he would put money. Oh— I don't know where he got it, but, we kept a discreet distance, watching from beneath a weeping willow, hiding as best we could behind the trunk.

"Bosco went to the edge of the monkey enclosure, where he found his son huddled in the corner, shivering. Bosco's wife, Orange Peel, ran to Bosco and they embraced through the bars. He kissed her and began tearing off pieces of chicken, feeding her through the bars. That's when things went terribly wrong.

"Shin Bone came out of the monkey shelter and caught them. He ran over and bit Orange Peel and dragged her into the monkey shack, beating her along the way. Bosco gripped the bars between them, helpless. What else could he do? He has no teeth, you know."

I heard Sarah gasp. "I didn't know. Why doesn't he have any teeth?"

"That's another story. Anyway, he was on the outside and they were on the inside. Bosco turned back and looked at Uncle Solomon—mortified. As it turned out, he must have known we were there the whole time. It was Bosco's eyes that sank my heart. His lips parted, his eyes grimaced, pleading. I leaned forward, convinced he was on the verge of asking me to remove the padlock on Orange Peel's cage.

"'This is why I never stay,' Uncle Solomon said as he wiped tears away. 'You are watching the disintegration of a man's family.' I realized Uncle Solomon had seen all this before.

"I'm sure if you asked him, Uncle Solomon would blame me for asking him to go."

"Good for him," Zoe said. "His sentiments are old-fashioned, the work of a vigilant mother, no doubt."

A *Jewish* mother, I thought. But, this was my stage. Not a time to get into Uncle Solomon's personal problems. "Shin Bone ran out of his shelter and grabbed Bosco's son. He slung him high in the air. The poor little monkey hit the earth hard and rolled to the opposite side of the cage. Shin Bone ran back inside the monkey shack, preventing Orange Peel from coming out, and doing who-knows-what to her. Nevertheless, it sounded terrible.

"Bosco must have died a little, taking all this in, a husband watching the destruction of what used to be his family. That's when I realized, Bosco hadn't given up. He lived in a conflicted binary star system. His heart revolved around his wife and son. Every free minute brought him back to his first love—which wasn't racing.

"I followed Bosco's eyes. They were locked on the dusty little fur ball, lifeless, unmoving. Bosco leaned forward, worrying, like any father would. He beckoned his son. The little guy just lay there. Was he alive? For the longest time, I couldn't tell. Finally, the baby raised his head, but refused to go to his father."

"Oh," Sarah gasped, on the verge of tears. "Boys feed on victory as much as food."

"Girls too," I said.

Sarah tilted her head. "I thought you said Bosco had a son?"

I felt Zoe stop rubbing my foot. I turned around and gave her a wicked glare, until she started rubbing again.

Sarah must have caught the exchange, because she too resumed her vigorous rubbing. "A boy's heart can die with too many defeats," she said, matter-of-factly. "Fathers are inscrutable sources of victory for sons."

She stopped rubbing my foot and leaned forward, trying to catch my eye. "Fathers shape the way sons interpret victory."

I grew weary of the *Father* subject. "Nevertheless—"

"To be a father is one of the most important roles a man is given to change the world." Sarah carped, on and on, her arms making sweeping gestures. "Anyone can raise a soldier, but after the bloodlust, the only cure for a warrior is to farm the earth, take a wife, educate his children, raise future trailblazers who will transform the lives of countless generations."

"All right, all right." I pointed to my foot, until she resumed my massage. "You're right about one thing, there was a hole in the baby's heart where his father should have been." I brought the back of my hand to my forehead. "This world is an unrelenting taskmaster that makes a father pedal a bike instead of being his son's advocate—and sons need an advocate." I stole a glance from beneath my wrist. Both were listening intently.

"Bosco's son must have known he once had a father and mother. He must have known they once loved him . . . then came this stranger, Shin Bone. Though Bosco's son could still see his father, he was no longer at the center of Bosco's world. A son, yes, but lost and separated, adrift, a rogue comet, confused, without an orbit, without a father, cold as ice, hurtling through a dark universe."

"Except he was a monkey," Zoe inserted.

"Just rub my foot," I said, pointing. "Eventually, Bosco's son limped over and curled up near Bosco. He laid there, weak, under-fed, losing his confidence with every passing day. How could he know his father was a champion racer? How could he know his future might be brighter than any other monkey in the zoo? And Bosco was helpless to show him. If only the baby could hang on a little longer.

"His father tore the chicken into small pieces, encouraging his son to eat. Bosco's face: that's the image I want cut from my memory. The saddest soul I've ever seen. What killed me was the slight smile he kept for his son. He was just a monkey, yet he knew his smile was the last thread of encouragement he could leave for his son—more important than the chicken.

"That's what he was doing when I made Uncle Solomon take me away. When I reached the car, I burst into tears. Bosco's son was stuck in that cage—with Shin Bone. How hopeless. His son is bound to give up. He'll die of a broken heart, I just know it."

I felt Zoe's little hand pat my leg, her version of reassurance.

"I felt guilty, leaving Bosco there—without a friend. As we drove away, I asked Uncle Solomon when Bosco would leave, how long would he sit with his son? He didn't answer at first. I had to ask a second time. Finally, he said, 'Until race time. He stays until race time.' Isn't that the saddest story you've ever heard?"

"No," said Sarah. "You did say that Bosco was a monkey, didn't you?"

I sat up. "Of course he is."

"Well then, let's not lose perspective. A monkey is not a thing to ruin your day."

Zoe tugged on Sarah's sleeve. "Girl hormones."

"It's not girl hormones!" I grabbed clumps of my hair, on the verge of tearing my hair out in frustration. "God help us if you get into medicine, with your girl-hormone theory."

What's the use? Sarah inhabits dreams and talks to angels. I frequent gambling halls and talk to chimps.

"Why is everyone ganging up on me? My day was ruined." I pulled my feet out of their grip and curled into a ball, refusing to look at them. I wasn't sure why I was punishing them. They hadn't hurt me. It's rather frightening to become a scold. I fear spitefulness will change my face, in a way that my inner ugliness will show outwardly.

I felt a hand stroke my hair. I heard Zoe whisper to Sarah, "I'll brush her hair and you do her nails."

"It's an unforgiving existence out there," Sarah said. "Come, sit at your vanity. Let me and Zoe erase everything terrible. We'll love and pamper you, so you can forget about the world's ugliness.

"I don't know why no one told you, your poor little monkey will have to find his own way. When mean-old Shin Bone dies, the baby will have an unobstructed view of a new world. If life has taught him anything, he'll bury his hurts. His mother must have instilled some coping skills. Mothers do, you know.

Mothers see the angel in their boys. Mothers may not be entirely right, but they see something. The rest is for sons to figure out, to find their better angel. Maybe sons everywhere struggle with this suffering. Who can say? Sons must learn that the worst kind of fear isn't what makes them scream, but what steals their voice and keeps them silent.

"Show a little faith," she sighed with great exaggeration.

I love Sarah, but she didn't understand. Who would have thought that Bosco's son was the only person who understood how I felt? Don't ask me about Iran or monkeys. I know, somewhere, a better world is out there. I'm locked in a nation of ignorance, listening to near-sighted tutors who teach *The Rubiyat*, as if every page had mythical importance.

Everyone knows Omar Khayyam is no prophet, but poetry is Persia's favorite sedative. My teachers probably haven't had an authentic thought in decades. They memorize poetry, patriotic chants, and recite prayers. Persians prefer perfume in place of ointment. So, our wounds never heal.

There I sat, a sister on each side, tending to beauty that no one appreciated, trapped in the Delkash compound while Armand was out there living his last days, eating his last meals, gambling on Bosco's final races.

Some things just don't fit . . . like me, in Iran.

Sixteen

I wait impatiently outside the Monkey Bar for my dawdling soldier-to-be. Three stories of brick, steel, magic, and monkey business. With its dark windows the average villager has no idea of all the fun inside. Armand is inside, probably bracing for future battles. My Achaemenes, my Ardashir, my Zhayedan. He will never admit this, but he frets desperately for our great nation.

My dear Armand is up to his neck in angst and patriotism. The devil of war had long ago taken hold of him. Teeming with itch and dissatisfaction, Armand has become a man of wagers; a boy watching monkey races; a youth unfamiliar with spiritual happiness . . . at least not his own. No, Armand is bred for a soldier's life of rescuing and heroics. As I think about it, that would fit nicely on a poster. I'm sure his future political campaign managers will leverage those sentiments.

I'm not silly. There is another way of life beyond Iran's solemn routines. Lately, I've reconnected with giggles that have been missing for years. Now that they're back, I'm slaphappy. Let me have my ecstasy. Some of us still find ways to make fire with a wet log. Girls too weak to follow their own dreams try to dampen mine. I had never considered girls as repressive, but having thought about it, school girls often create self-doubt—deliberately. It's part of the Mean Girl culture coming from the West.

Death to America.

Let my so-called friends wag their tongues. While doubters debate matches made in heaven, I'll embrace mine—no thanks to them. Why are girls so quick to give advice that's better applied to themselves? I guess it never occurs to them—I never asked. Little do they realize, I already know the answer, I just don't want to hear it. I can't explain why, but my heart heeds the migration call coming from *gay Paree*. I need an emergency transplant to Paris.

Birds build their nests in the strangest places. Sarah uses this phrase to prove a point about women who marry unsuitable men. *Oh, Jamileh. Love is so inherently preposterous. Ninety percent of infatuation is projecting imaginary fancies on some poor unsuspecting soul. Whoever survives your x-rayed, gamma-rayed, misguided attention will deserve a medal.*

We'll see about that. The next hour will be me, severing ties with a house full of tattle-tits, and rejecting all their unsolicited advice. Even Giti complains that I over exaggerate how good something will be, to the extent it could never measure up to my descriptions. Ava tells me that marriage is a long con. *Don't be so anxious*, she says, with her refined French accent.

They're all wrong about Armand. Common sense is always better than a committee—a committee of estrogen, jealousy, and gossip.

No matter. I intend to escape this port city's domestic embargo on love. The next hour will be me, making plans with the wrongly accused, the haphazardly condemned. *Armand.*

Knowing Armand, he'll probably be on his way to another festivity, so my opportunity to save him will be fleeting. The afternoon sun wanes to the west— always toward France. Shopkeepers are slashing their prices to clear out the morning's inventory. The marketplace is always a clockwork of opportunities. Afternoons create sad merchants posting reduced prices and joyful shoppers carting away in bulk.

Here I stand, waiting, on the periphery of the business district, but still near the hubbub of buying and selling, invisible to distracted shoppers, one step removed from a dust-up of seven quarrelsome languages, babbling in blinkered prosy cons.

Standing in front of the Monkey Bar is no safe zone for toes. I frequently step aside as donkeys pull carts with abscising wooden wheels.

It's odd, but I haven't felt my community's heartbeat in months. Now that my departure is imminent, I don't mind savoring its unique bouquet of sights, and aromas—since this could be my last opportunity.

Much as I suspect, Armand exits the Monkey Bar, loud, boisterous, yelling off-color farewells to his so-called friends still seated inside. He stumbles out to the street, still laughing, still irreverent.

I run up to him, until I match his gait, step for step. "*Psst*. Armand!"

He turns slowly, staring with a drug-addled expression. He squints cocking his head—nothing but simmering question marks re-shape his face.

"Follow me," I say.

"But—"

"*Shh!* To the benches in front of the Caviar Shop, but sit behind me, back to back. I have something important to tell you. We can't let the Basij accuse us of consorting."

It does startle me that he complies so willingly. My heart tightens with every step. A new sense of power washes over me. I can't help but smile, walking with a little more bounce of authority. Though Armand is fit as any king to reign in Iran, he obeys me. *Me.* This is probably how much of our married life will be. Sure, his friends think he's a wild socialite, but the two of us will wink at each other knowing that he looks to me for approval and direction. My insightful leadership will probably become his secret weapon.

As I sit, I hear the bench behind me squeak. I turn to make sure it's him—just in case. We're safe. This is, after all, a public place, a place for meeting, purchasing, and swindling. People not so different from us come and go. The two of us are just typical people on a typical day in Noshahr. No need for all these glancing eyes to be suspicious. Still, I watch cautiously.

I clutch my purse with both hands and clear my throat. "I was raised on patriotic duty to Iran. So, don't take this as disrespect for your national aspirations, but I have an airline ticket to Paris . . . for you."

He didn't answer. In the delay, my feet tapped with the same nervous adrenaline that causes a driver to rev his engine. I reached in my purse and pulled out my three tickets. Whatever he decides—even if I must run—at least I had two more tickets for me and Giti. Had he misunderstood my intent?

"Aaand—" he queried, sliding heavy on the opening vowel.

"I have one too. Don't move. I'll drop your ticket beside you." I looked both ways for Basij. When the coast was clear, I dropped his ticket on his side of the bench. I heard the envelope *crinkle* and *shoosh*. I wondered if he objected to American Airlines. If he was reading the ticket, he sure was taking his time.

"You mean, instead of military duty?"

"Yes." I said with unintentional sass. Maybe he thought me traitorous. "I'm not suggesting wrongdoing, but do you think Sharia Law condones Iran battling Iraq, Muslim fighting Muslim? What must Allah think?"

An officer of the Basij appeared. He carried a small fish bat that he twirled as he strolled through the crowd. I must have done something to catch his attention. He moved in my direction and stared directly into my eyes. He used his bat to move my hands away from my purse. He scowled at its logo, Yves Saint Laurent. Shaking his head, he ambled down the street, barely interested in the offenses that surrounded him.

I heard Armand exhale, as if he had held his breath the whole time. "That kind of talk could get you erased, me erased—me and all memory of my existence. The Secret Police will see to that."

Armand did not take my words. He was much too eager with assertions. "Don't forget," I reminded him, "Ayatollah Khomeini stayed in Paris while he waited for Iran to sort itself out."

Another long pause. I sensed his inner conflict, but easy answers don't exist in Iran. "And what will the war do to you?" I asked. "I don't mean to frighten, but this current administration is unraveling. Maybe you were meant for better things."

"My ticket is for a commercial flight . . . out of Azerbaijan," he complained.

"Mine too. No airport in Iran would permit us to leave. I'm under-aged and without proper documentation. And you . . . leaving might be construed as desertion."

"What's your name, again?" Disconcerting wonder suffused his question.

He didn't even know my name. Birds stopped singing. The wind from the Caspian Sea ceased. Earth no longer orbited the Sun. If people were nearby, I didn't sense them. "Jamileh, Jamileh Delkash."

"Oh, Sarah's sister."

"Yes." Near laughter, it occurred to me, I'd grown into womanhood faster than his mind could register. *Could this woman be the same girl I crushed so hard on all those years ago?* he must have thought.

"Is Sarah going?"

"No."

Armand exhaled with the same relief I'd witnessed from passengers disembarking a ferry, after a scary ride on a choppy sea. "Oh hell, it's not like I haven't thought about this." He sighed as though a great weight had lifted from his shoulders. "But, why are *you* going to Paris?"

My first reaction? Anguish. I was hoping for excitement at the prospect of traveling with me—or better yet, that he would playfully introduce the word *elope* into our conversation. But, such a topic veered too close to a woman's virtue. The word *runaway*, when describing an Iranian girl, bristled with apostasy and unbridled sexuality. An image decent women quickly rebut.

"As for my ticket, I see a new door opening. I've already contacted French universities about a proper curriculum in hydroponics. I'm not running from a nightmare. I'm chasing a dream, through foreign education. I suspect we both are. At least we can console one another while in exile—being fellow Persians, and all."

He swatted his ticket against his palm, absentmindedly. "I'm not sure I'll be up to any studies. Where are the travel permits?"

"No travel permits. I haven't worked out all the details."

"We couldn't get past the border guards without permits."

He certainly had a knack for putting his finger on my glitch. "Do you have friends with diplomatic plates? I haven't filled in all the gaps, but in a worst-case scenario, Ava Herat has offered to get us across the northern border."

"Ava?" Armand moaned. "Stay away from Ava."

"Do you have any political connections traveling to Azerbaijan?"

"My friends don't cross through border guards," he said.

"What do you mean?"

"The rich never fly commercial." His complaint was framed in barbed wire. "Anyone who knows anything about travel, knows a private jet is the only way to come and go from Iran. No travel permits, no border guards, no hassle."

Rude.

I had to think that one through, insult and all. "Well, I don't have a private jet." I knew as soon as the words left my mouth our family wasn't rich. Uncle Solomon's low-minded assessment of our social status had cost me my dignity. *Off to a good start* Uncle Solomon had said.

Ha!

"Okay," he said. "Your tickets are for the end of the week. What if we can't make the flight?"

"I don't want to think in such negative terms, but plane tickets are cheap. Price is the least of my concerns. Our problem is getting past the northern border guards. Maybe you know a shady character with a solution or two?"

I heard him flicking his ticket as he thought. "Conscription is bad news any way I look at it. Many friends never made it back from the border wars. Allah enrolled them in the noble army of martyrs. Blessed be Allah and His honorable prophet. The ones who did make it back, didn't return with all their parts."

"War has a way of resolving itself," I said in a softer, kinder voice. "This war doesn't need you. What difference can one more soldier make? Come away.

After a few years, you can return with credentials—an education that will better Iran."

"My father is an educated man," Armand moaned, "but you wouldn't know it to look at him. Everyone here wears the same Islamic death shroud. No one in Europe took him seriously in his white, buttoned-up salwar kameez, and he has a Ph.D. I was raised in Paris, but born in Iran—which has become nothing more than the rotting remains of Persia. A relic."

My spine straightened in disbelief. "Do you believe that—hand on heart?"

"Yes. I've always hated Iran." Armand spoke in a rickety voice, still quivering. "A few of us talked about flying down to Morocco and smoking out the remainder of the war."

I had no idea Armand felt like this. Why didn't *he* buy a ticket? Where was *his* initiative?

"Thank you, Jamileh. You took a big risk. I'll make it up to you. You have my word."

Butterflies.

I had his word. He was forming a pact, a new bond, him being the promisor and me being the promisee. This moved our swiftly evolving relationship closer toward a *flirtationship*. My love was growing by leaps . . . and there were no bounds! I wanted to kiss him, and I know he wanted to kiss me.

When girls go out in public they shouldn't be forced to leave their hearts at home. Hammering heartbeats were reshaping me, *thump* by *thump*.

You have my word, he said. We shared a secret.

It's times like these when a girl, like me, living in oppression must take whatever madness is offered, to see beyond the dark jailer of Islam.

And Mother is with me again, like an unshakeable ear worm, singing her entreaty: *take a ring, take another, and a necklace too, if that won't do*.

My heart was in a flurry, like one of those snow globes with an Eiffel Tower inside. Little bits of glittering snowflakes blinded me with lovemania. The moment was full of omens and envisionings. I was literally seeing flashing runway lights—landing gear down.

Even without a kiss, everything was perfect. I was conflicted, knowing a kiss would get us locked up. But, a hug? I turned to wrap my arms around him . . . but he was gone.

Seventeen

"Armand will take his father's official vehicle," I explained to Giti. "It has diplomatic plates. The airport in Baku is only a three-hour drive, so, no need for forged documents. As the son of our French Ambassador, with his father's car, he can speed us through any border stop."

Aghast, Giti closed the orphanage gate and led me a few steps away, out of foot traffic, out of earshot. She towered over me, her face in full grimace. "What about our plans for Hollywood?"

"That was your plan. My heart has always belonged to Paris, the city of love, the land of liberty. You'll be safe with me. Tonight's the night, Giti. Armand has it all worked out. He'll pick you up, here, in front of the orphanage, at eleven . . . and you can't be a minute late. Then, you two will come for me. I'll be waiting near our compound, on the paved government road."

"He won't show up," Giti huffed. "You don't know the Armand I know. You see him once a month, at a distance. I see him every day. He quit school, can't keep a job, his father threw him out of the house, and Armand never pays his gambling debts. He's a bully to the weak, and a cowering collaborator to the Secret Police . . . and maybe he's already informed on you.

"He should have stayed in France. He's a French libertine who returned to corrupt our godly way of life, hiding behind smooth European manners, but that leech has the morals of a parasite. An emotionless gamester, playful eyes, cold heart—and shame on you for considering such a man who lives off others."

"And who lives off the orphanage?"

"But I sew for my room and board. A person willing to work and pay their own way can take pride in that, even if they can't take pride in anything else. Armand sponges off everyone who crosses his path. Too many girls marry that sort of man. A trap of gossamer and murky wishes. Girls never notice until his steel jaws are firmly impaled in their flesh, far too late to run."

I tilted my head, wondering if I'd misunderstood her. "Who's running?"

"You are—in the wrong direction—from a loving family."

I *humphed* and folded my arms. "You've never liked Armand."

"I've seen worse men, but you covet this fool, and all consequences be damned."

"How could you presume to know what I want and don't want?"

She grabbed my shoulders and gave me a shake. "Wake up, Jamileh. Take those designer boots off and stand barefoot in the stardust-speckled dirt with your face up to the throne of Allah. There is so much more to this moment—this day. Forget Hollywood. Stay here with me. Iran has enough life in it for generations to come. I'm your friend. He's not husband material. I'm telling you this as someone who cares about you. Don't go near that car thief, that two-faced coward."

"I suppose an orphan like you would refuse a proposal from the son of an ambassador."

"Yes." She nodded emphatically.

"You'll never have the privilege of being asked. So, don't pretend you have options that don't exist—Princess Giti."

Why does Giti make me say such horrible things? I want adventure so badly it's making me bad-tempered, and Giti lacks the education to hear the freedoms beckoning beyond Iran's borders.

I leaned against the warm brick wall that surrounded the orphanage, exasperated. "What would it take to convince you, Giti? You have nothing holding you here. I don't either. I woke up today with another anguished sigh and Father's never-ending to-do lists. Try dealing with that. It made me want to pull the covers back over my head. All this shopping, planning, and practice-packing. I'm exhausted. That's why I need you. I would have asked my sisters to help me set up my Paris apartment, but they don't know I'm leaving."

Giti sighed as if I was someone to pity. "Maybe your problem is, you really don't have a problem."

I couldn't believe my ears. "Are you talking to me? You don't know anyone with bigger problems than me."

"Oh, Jamileh, this is so risky. You'll always have a place to come back to. If I'm not at morning roll call, a new girl gets my bed."

"Giti, I've made my decision. You have to come with me to Paris."

"No offense, but your plans change more often than the days of the week."

"That's an exaggeration. I've already bought your ticket." I took her hand and slapped her palm with an envelope emblazoned with a logo: American Airlines.

God bless America.

Her eyes widened to huge circles. "You've thought of everything. Western American Airlines. I bet they'll serve automatic coffee and speak English. I'll get to use my English sentence when we disembark: 'See you later alligator.'"

At this point, I knew I had someone to keep me company . . . at least until my wedding. "And I'll say: '*Adieu.*'"

Giti turned gravely serious and clasped both my hands. "I have a confession. I'm afraid of travel. I could never survive in a world I knew nothing about. On the other hand, if you left me, I have no other friends. Not one."

Not much of a confession. I already knew her begging made her the village pariah.

"For you, I would take this risk." As she mouthed these words, her eyes misted. "Me, on an airplane. Are you sure? Nothing this grand has ever happened to me. This seems too big, too wonderful."

I nodded and pointed west, toward Paris. "By the weekend, you and I will picnic along the Seine River, the way we used to picnic along the Caspian Sea. And there's more. I'm bringing my inheritance to purchase a small apartment. So, we won't have to worry about a place to stay."

Giti stepped back, gasping. Finally, she realized I was serious. "Let there be bread, water, and salt for all. Have you ever noticed there are two jokers in every deck of cards? That's all I want, to be shuffled into something wonderful, to be part of *something*, even if I'm nothing."

"You and your improbable monsters. In Paris we'll be something. We're about to find out what it means to be a woman in Paris. I'll learn what event marks the transition into womanhood, with a capital *W*. I'm ready to grow up. What line do I stand in? See! I don't even know where the line is."

I have a destiny as certain as my next breath. I now realize that Armand needs me, the way Wednesday needs Tuesday. Everything makes sense. A man needs a woman. Rather primitive, but it's as natural as a snow melt finding its channel downhill. Suddenly, I'm part of the heartbeat of humanity. I care for a man and he loves . . . cares . . . or at the very least, notices me."

*   *   *

This is my toes-over-the-cliff moment. I stand in my room gazing down at my suitcase, facing a frightening realization: tonight, I fly. I'd practiced

packing many times—imagining. As awful as it
sounds, I'm about to be a runaway girl.

One London Fog carry-on traveler with wheels—
Soho Collection. It contains my best skirts, blouses,
and silky French underthings.

No headscarves. I'll take one Islam-appropriate
outfit, but, when I land in Paris, off comes the
headscarf . . . and everything else that reeks of the
Middle-East. I realize I'm somewhat less observant
than I thought. Sarah would call that, *A Muslimah with
negotiable virtues*. It's painful to justify every little
thing to my big sister. Details give me a headache.

As I step outside our house, the night air is nippy,
but I press on. When I reach the gate, my hand refuses
to slide back the iron latch.

Guilt.

I park my carry-on and give the secret
compartment a pat, in tribute to Mother. I had shopped
for days to find something with a secret compartment,
to hide her two rings and pearl necklace. I lean against
our gate's stone arch, dithering. I couldn't leave—yet.

A brief note is the fair thing to do, for a family
who've done me no wrong. I return inside, tip-toe up
the spiral staircase, and into my room. I collect a sheet
of paper and pen—a Mont Blanc. I close my eyes,
straining for the words to pen my farewell. In school,
we studied the natural form of a married woman's
correspondence. She normally includes her domestic
complaints, how powerless she feels in the winds of
fate, worked-to-the-bone, and sad. I suppose I'll need
to address my feelings so I won't appear ungrateful.

Dear Father, I imagine. *Why don't you love me anymore?* Ooh, that felt weird. What a silly thought. Yet, it nearly brings me to tears. Suddenly, I'm overwhelmed with bitterness and resentment. I'm not sure why. I come from a good home—a loving family.

Every parent has their own take on training daughters to be appreciative. But what parents never realize, kids leave. If I'm lucky I'll survive backstabbers, broken hearts, failures, and all the hidden pressures of modern fashion. Even smart kids make stupid decisions. I'm not afraid. I'm ready to make mine.

Parents need to recognize the vast probability that their kids might become victims of this age—this complicated era. You can't blame daughters for being unsatisfied with what they have. Every generation should strive to better itself. So, I write.

Dear Father,

Don't worry about me. I'm with very honorable friends. You might read about me in the newspapers. If they take pictures you'll see how happy my face looks (the wind blows a lot in France, so, don't jump to conclusions if my headscarf has blown off).

You were probably too busy driving around with Uncle Solomon to notice my work at the orphanage, but volunteering was a big part of my life. Volunteering was a *huge* part of my life! If I was a bit older I could have settled all this properly, but the safety of Giti being foremost on my mind, prevented me from doing so.

This matter will resolve itself in a few years. And, yes, I will enroll in school, immediately. The next time you see me, I'll have my credentials in aqua engineering—an important skill for bettering the world.

Maybe you, Sarah, and Zoe can join me in Paris. I've learned the ins and outs of escaping Iran. As it turns out, it's not that hard, when you know the right people.

Sarah and I have spent our entire lives watching you leave. We don't know what *go* feels like. I only came and went when you required it. Tonight, my future requires it. I still haven't the ability to articulate all the details, but I must go.

Salam

Jamileh

I place my farewell letter in the center of my bed and line it up to match the edges. A perfect paper rectangle on a larger cotton rectangle. I step quickly from my room, so as not to shed a tear, to leave with nary a regret.

I close my door for the last time, but like a weakling, I put my forehead against the door jamb and close my eyes.

"You look like Ava," comes Sarah's voice.

I jump back in a startle. At the end of the hallway, Sarah steps from the shadows, ghostly and upset. Her eyes are firm, judgmental.

"They call that *Persianality*, my backward sister."

"Pastiche," she says with a sneer. "Be yourself.

Be what no one else can: you. If you drape yourself in Western fabrics, you surrender. Make your own statement, because those extravagant clothes will overtalk you. Don't be Ava."

Self-conscious, I fasten my jilbab jacket. "Not tonight, Sarah."

"I had a dream," she says.

"Go back to your dreams." Despite her seniority, how little she understands. I have my own dreams. Two plane tickets in my pocket and Paris in my heart. Father would soon show her my note and perfectly-made bed. What a cruel thing, as I think about it. Sarah is the best sister I could ask for. Yet, despite her kindness, I couldn't risk sharing tonight's details.

"I dreamt of locks snapping shut and latches slamming," she says. "In this dream, it wasn't Father locking up. It was you."

How I want to laugh out loud, but how helpless I feel. I can't put her mind at ease, because I'm moments away from *unlocking* and *unlatching*. But, I won't let her agonize for long—no more than a week or two. I'll post her the very night I arrive in Paris. Then, by letter, I'll explain about Armand and me. "Don't worry about me. I go nowhere unless I'm under the safe wings of a guardian."

"Not tonight," she says, deadly earnest.

She's ignoring me, but as the younger sister, I'm used to it. "I have to go. Don't worry."

"I'll set something out," she says "to warm your feet . . . a heated soapstone. You can wrap it in a soft towel when you return. Stay safe my little sister." She steps back into the darkness, vanishing like an apparition, leaving only the faint sound of her door closing.

Weird.

I dash downstairs, my first flush of f-r-e-e-d-o-m. I slip through our front door, without re-locking. Outside, I grab my luggage, swing open the front gate, without re-latching, and leave. I'll be long gone, but the first lesson Father will learn tomorrow morning is that no harm came to his precious house. His locks and latches were inconsequential, and his teacher—me— will be in Paris. *You're welcome, good sir.* Sometimes I can outshine the fox in cleverness.

I trudge through the sand, stopping and tugging at my carry-on. I leave two thin lines behind me, evidence of high hopes, poor traction, and exhaustion. My long skirt is getting dusty and I'm breathing harder.

These wheels are useless without the flooring of a department store. I struggle and jerk at the handle. Thank goodness Mother's jewels are safely tucked away in a hidden compartment. The British are so clever at creating undiscoverable compartments. I've read enough Ian Fleming to know that much.

I stand on the side of the road for . . . what seems like forever . . . at least ten minutes, waiting for Armand. The darkness is full of unfamiliar noises. How I long to see the stately car belonging to Armand's father. How I yearn for its majestic arrival, with its formidable headlights that project out for miles.

I suppose Armand knows how to drive. I hope he
knows how to drive. Normally, I can see his father's
car coming from miles away. Nothing tonight except a
few random gunshots in the distance. I hope he
remembers to turn on the headlights.

I'm sitting on *G* waiting on *O*.

Strange characters walk past and gawk, night
creatures scurry across the road, occasionally a strange
car passes and slows. I decide to walk toward the
orphanage, since Armand is probably only minutes
away. The wheels of my carry-on don't work well on
Iranian asphalt. Unless Armand comes quickly, I fear
they will break and come off.

Where is Armand?

How odd I must appear to onlookers, a young
woman, alone at night. I hear a vehicle approaching
behind me. I turn. Cutting through a thin cloud of
ground fog, a Mercedes van appears in the distance—
not Armand. The large van's rattling diesel engine
comes close enough that I fear it will run me over. I
move to the far edge of the road. A girl could get hit.
Devils are active in these late hours.

Unfortunately, the van shows interest in my
plight. It passes, but I hear the loud sneeze of airbrakes
as it stops a short distance ahead. I turn in the opposite
direction, back toward home, not knowing what
mischief the driver has in mind. As it backs toward me
I increase my pace. I gauge the running distance back
home. Too far. This van-load of who-knows-what
closes in fast. I drop my luggage and run flat out, heels
notwithstanding.

"*Bonjour!*" I hear Ava's voice call out.

I turn, half-humiliated, half-relieved. "What are you doing here?"

"Armand could not get da car. Jump in."

Eighteen

The van smelled funny, poor-people funny. But, when I sat next to Ava, my eyes shut tight, triggered by a childhood memory. Ava wore the same Noora Perfume Mother wore, a much-needed respite in these cramped quarters.

Like Mother, Ava was the only one who looked after me; the only one who knew what my next step should be . . . even before I did. I was on my way. I was warm. I was aglow with appreciation.

I reached over and stroked Ava's camel-hair jilbab. "Such soft material, dignified, and sophisticated." I squared my fingers, photo-frame style. "You're a paragon of Islamic fashion."

Ava wasn't the smiling type, but my imaginary photoshot caused a grin she couldn't repress. "Nobody wants a night out unless dey outshine da other girls." She looked toward the back of the van and made a show of being irritated that everyone was envying her.

Maybe she was right. I for one wished I had worn something as nice as hers. Saying Ava was full of herself made no sense to my way of thinking. I've never understood that idiom. Who else would she be full of?

What an enchanted evening. We were both more gorgeous than ever.

The bench seats behind us were filled with girls from God-only-knows-where. I had almost forgotten about Giti, but there she was, seated in the far back.

She fit right in. No fashion, no hygiene. She kept waving her dirty nails at me—desperate at times. She pointed at the driver.

May Allah forgive my murderous thoughts, but the driver was that creep from the Monkey Bar, the whiffy Ava shooed away after he dropped gold coins on our table. I should have known. Nothing but a driver.

After we arrived at the shoreline, we were unloaded. I didn't intend to humiliate anyone, but I did smirk after noticing no one else packed. They parted like the Red Sea as I walked through them, pulling my new London Fog, carry-on. I raised my chin, irritated that everyone was envying me.

Giti rushed to join me. She spoke like a frenzied metronome, on and on, out it poured. Every sentence lost more and more focus until it ended with no resemblance of the subject she began with. She ended with the oddest declarations: ". . . and Armand was drunk and refused to come!" For years, I thought I wasn't paying sufficient attention. But it was her—the whole time.

Scatterbrained.

Our group continued northbound, walking toward Azerbaijan. Supposedly, we had an arrangement to meet a bus with a heater. We were coming to the edge of hill country, with steep ridges plunging down to the rocky shoreline. Giti droned on and on, stumbled, waved her arms, but always spoke in whispers with wide-eyed exaggerations. "I waited where you told me," she said. "I waited for Armand at the time you specified—even after I heard he joined the Basij. That's how his father got him a deferment. I waited despite friends telling me they were on their way to celebrate with Armand. I waited until the Whore of Babylon came along and told me Armand sent her, to pick you up."

Giti had a knack for saying exactly what I didn't want to hear. "That is a lie," I said. "Armand would never join the Basij. That's lower than a soldier."

"But nowhere near as dangerous," she said defensively. Then she made her eyes look like they felt sorry for me.

I verged on giving her a good face slap. "Number one, he wouldn't stoop that low; number two, he would have invited me; number three, he would never leave me alone on the street, waiting. He would never— Mark my word, he'll soon be here. Then we'll get on with his original plan."

The whiffy with the Pashtun cap caught up with us and tried to walk next to me. He bowed with great ceremony, so excessively polite I suspected he had endured many humiliations in his life.

"Buzz off, hat boy." I thought it best not to encourage him.

"What did I do?" He said it like I had hurt his feelings, as if he deserved to walk next to me.

"Go wash camels, or whatever it is that you do. You're not needed here."

"I do not wash camels," he whined, followed by a shriveled pout.

The persistent driver just couldn't take a hint. Again, I attempted to dissuade the pest. "In a universe of matter, anti-matter, and dark-matter, you've cornered the market on don't matter."

"Ah, but tonight you will need me. So, I do matter. After we switch vehicles, I will be the driver taking you north. You can count on that, one-hundred-and-fifty percent."

"I'm sorry. Did I accidentally roll my eyes out loud? I'm tremendously *not* sorry that my intelligent sense of humor offended your utter lack of it."

I switched sides of the path and placed Giti between us. My Italian Valentinos were unsuited for actual walking, and I was tiring of his poor attempts at conversation. I tried to get Ava's attention, but she was too far ahead of us. I intended to have her dismiss this pest, *without pay*.

After many minutes of struggling with my carry-on, I gasped for breath in an unbecoming way. Ball bearings and Iranian sand were a lethal combination for London Fog wheels.

I looked around and realized the Pashtun driver was walking empty handed. I stepped in front of him and shook a finger in his face. "What kind of driver makes a woman carry her own luggage?"

His eyes brightened as he glanced down at my luggage. "Well, excuse me, sheikha Jamileh." He kindly took the handle, lifted my bag over his head . . . and heaved it into the gulley!

Mother's rings— Mother's necklace— My tuition— My Paris apartment—

I staggered, speechless. My hands covered my mouth as my luggage rolled end-over-end down the hill. "You contemptible pig!" I looked around for a large stick to beat him with.

He laughed, jumped behind Ava, and taunted me with goofy faces and insulting hand gestures.

"March down there and get it," I commanded.

He wagged his head, glowing with an obnoxious smirk.

I turned to Ava. "This is not endurable. Have this man whipped."

Ava glared down at me. "No time." She trudged onward.

I continued to grab around Ava, swiping at the driver. "Everything I had was in that bag. Scurry down that hill, you worthless *chos*."

Ava pushed me along. "Keep moving."

But my bag was still in sight. I planted both feet and folded my arms. "Not another step without my luggage."

Ava continued her unremitting march, but directed the driver to bring me along. He threw me over his shoulder and I watched my inheritance fade into the dark distance. Nothing had gone the way I planned it.

Plan B: As soon as I reach the airport I intend to charter a taxi, come back for my carry-on, and find Armand. Then I'll buy *new* tickets, and it's off to Paris.

I was so frustrated and uncomfortable as I dangled over the driver's shoulder. I bounced like wet laundry with his every step.

He stepped lively through knee-deep fog that rolled off the Caspian, proud of his dominance. After a short distance, everyone stopped, alerted to something just ahead. Almost in unison, they all leaned toward a sound. The Pashtun driver set me on my own two feet. He too reacted to the distant rumble.

Making out shapes beneath the full moon wasn't a problem. I saw a number of cargo vans—three. Three metal behemoths lumbered and rattled. Behind the headlights of each boxy vehicle, came a strange mix of contradictory noises, some mechanical, some animal. As they came nearer, their drivers were forced to get out to inspect a dangerous curve in the road. My blood ran cold. I knew an Afghan warlord when I saw one.

I breathed easier knowing I had Ava as my protector.

As their engines idled down, I could finally make out the other sounds that had puzzled me: whimpers and sobs, of the female sort.

One man from our group lit his lantern and waved it to the three-truck caravan. A lantern from the other group waved in return. As the metal caravan advanced, I could make out faded Russian emblems on the drivers' doors. They had converted Russian war relics for their own evil deeds. Smuggling. And from the sound of it, tonight's cargo was young girls, hours away from being converted into cash for the Islamic war effort.

The formerly hospitable faces of the two men in our group lost their friendly. Their eyes, suddenly predatory, became nails that fixed me in place, daring me to run.

I worried for Ava. She had surrounded herself with unscrupulous men who were about to betray her.

After Ava's driver yelled to the caravan, I was certain. We were about to be sold to the larger group— wholesale, no doubt.

"Ava," I whispered. "I fear there are dark minds at play here." I gripped her arm, backing the two of us toward our most prudent escape . . . a dark ravine. After our escape, I intended to retrieve my carry-on, along with my inheritance.

Wordless, I bugged my eyes at Giti and gestured toward the ravine. But Giti had surmised all this long before me. She dashed like a black-tailed gazelle toward the ravine and ran as if her life depended on it.

A lone shot cracked the midnight air and Giti fell, clutching her thigh.

"Giti!" I grabbed Ava's sleeve, in shock.

Giti removed her headscarf to make a tourniquet. She turned to me with a woeful expression I will never forget. I was the one who convinced her to leave the orphanage. Her eyes told me this was my doing, but I had already reached the same conclusion. Giti was an innocent victim of my escapade.

The man who shot her turned his pistol in my direction. I stopped edging toward the ravine, stopped blinking, stopped breathing.

The captive girls from the other caravan were unloaded by enormous square men. I heard the guards tell them to stretch their legs and relieve themselves— right out in the open.

When the girls saw our group, it gave them false hope. They screamed for our help. How sad. I ached for them—for me.

Annoyed by the commotion, one of their heartless guards turned and threatened these poor waifs. The fist he raised would *wham* into some helpless girl and she would be silenced. A simple *shush* was not part of his vocabulary . . . I supposed.

This ghoulish parade of pale, bloodless bodies joined our group, more hopeless than ever. Moonlight caused an eerie bioluminescence beneath their pale skin. Their clothes sagged and flapped in the oddest places. Doubtless, when they were kidnapped, their clothes fit splendidly and went well together with their body. All their tears begged for a hug, but no hug was coming for these girls. Something else was coming— and it wasn't pretty.

"Who are they?" I heard my own idiotic voice ask. I knew who they were, and so did Ava. I guess that's what I do when I see an unavoidable disaster headed straight at me. I guess when my feet falter, all that remains is the lowest part of my brain that still runs my mouth. I felt blood drain from my expression, my posture lost its grip. I knew who they were, and though I couldn't bear the thought, I knew what lay ahead.

We were lined up and counted—all but Ava. The other girls quivered, shook, hiccupped, and bawled with demonic energy. I was tradable, commerce, a bulk commodity. An appalling sense of resignation swept through me. It was as if I left my body. I guess these things happen. It all came from the same constellation of fear.

I imagined my entire life spinning beneath me, disintegrating. I had made mistakes in my short lifetime, terrible mistakes, but this was horrendous. Armand had ruined my life. This night would completely, irreversibly, permanently, eternally, irredeemably, diminish my value to a potential husband, force me to reject reputable men, avoid the smile of decent men, lest they discover my dark secret: a bought and sold woman. I would be unworthy of a slot in proper society.

Even lepers know when to quarantine themselves.

I wanted to go home. Had I glimpsed a fraction of the suffering outside our walls, had I foreseen the risk, I would have helped Father with his evening lock-up. But that was when the world wasn't so scary and everything was orderly. That was when my father was bigger than life and not human.

In my defense, I didn't choose evil because I sought evil. I mistook it for happiness. People can change, but in my case, I don't think anyone will care. In the World to Come, I bet if we explained our lives to Allah, He would be shocked at how little we learned, and our misinterpretations of the whole mess. How little I knew. How incapable I was of knowing. By the time we understand what to ask, our opinions no longer matter.

It was all I could do to remain upright. I was in the process of fainting when one of Ava's men caught me. If only my mouth would work, I would protest.

So this was it? Is this where I became one of those poor Iranian girls who disappeared into the night? Odd, that I hadn't seen this coming. Odder yet that Giti had.

Giti limped over to me and used my shoulder to brace herself. "I thought you said Ava was your friend?"

I didn't even have the strength to defend myself. Maybe I was still lightheaded, but I thanked Ava for the adventure and asked if we could return to Noshahr.

"*Nyet*," she sneered. She'd lost that sweet lift in her voice. Our walking and the late hour had her in a frazzle. She couldn't even maintain the pretense of a French accent. Her Russian tongue was back, and sounded none too pretty. Giti had warned me about that too.

Nyet, she said. Too bad. The desire for my warm room had taken hold. I enjoyed that thought: a fire-warmed, towel-wrapped, soapstone under my feet. I needed that cordial thought to pacify myself, at least until we were sold.

"Look at it dis vay," Ava said, "start fresh. New people. New opportunities. Vith prostitution, you be anyone you vant."

I was taken aback as much by her emotionless delivery as the words themselves. A good friend once warned me that, one day, I would wane atavistic. As I watched my world slip away, I wanted it back. Young or old, there comes a time in everyone's life when a rescuing angel should appear. If only one would show up with a flower and a smile. No such angel for me.

"Jamileh?" Ava queried. "Iz der possibility dat you are upside-down vith all your thinking? Girls avoid social guilt by conforming. Always conforming. Prostitution vill be good for you."

Before I could sling back a barbed retort, the pike-end of her words assailed me. Maybe there was a nugget of truth in Ava's sick advice. Even among the most noisome prostitution dens in Tehran, there was something of a woman's original nature still intact. I would still be me . . . I desperately hoped.

"I take care of your vork—at least da first five years. Den, you can go to precious France."

It was all so terrible that I tuned her voice out. Not that she was speaking to me. More like she was in another zone, a conversation with herself that occasionally included me.

Ava had plotted to sell me from the beginning. I remembered that she wanted me to bring Sarah and Zoe. Now, it was all so clear. In her version of me, all she saw was an echo in a well—a nobody. She had spoken like she was doing *me* a favor, but to my ears it didn't sound like a favor at all.

The Russian trucks restarted their engines. Ava ordered all us girls to climb inside—with her new Russian accent.

I blocked Ava's path. "Stop! In the name of our friendship and all that is holy, you must stop this."

She reached back and delivered an unexpected slap that sent me spinning to the ground.

Nineteen

A slap.

My skull still rattles, the pain peals away, thinner and thinner. I lie in a sprawl. My brain throbs as I gaze up at Ava. She's just a blur.

Wallowing in dirt my fingers slide beneath me until I can prop myself up, then, I'm sitting aslant, in dirt, dusty and defeated. I remain, head hung low, brooding, a spectacle. The stinging memory still echoes on my skin. So, I press my cool palm against my burning cheek.

The face is a sacred place. A slap is a defacement, a despoiling. The principal suffering of the poor is indignity. Although I want nothing to do with it, indignity gathers me with its brawny arms, against my will. I don't know why I feel so weak, wretched, and wrong—only that I do. Before I could say *Pandora's Box*, I had been toppled, and not a soul stood up in my defense.

I'm careful not to look anyone in the face because I don't want them to see the shame in my eyes, and I don't want to see the laughter in theirs. Feelings go underground. With all eyes on me, I short-circuit, go numb—my only recourse. I have nothing else to say. Four words echo in my mind: *You silly little fool. You silly little fool. You silly little fool. . . .*

Humiliation sucks all the color out of my celebrity, leaving me ordinary, far from who I could have been. How will the intensity of this shame be understood by those who never experience it? My chest is so full of heartbeats that my brain has hiccups.

Now is my chance to lay it all on the table, but I
won't. That's the problem with shame. Shame doesn't
like company and shuns confrontation. Only an hour
earlier, I left my cozy bedroom. For this. I can't
forgive myself.

You silly little fool.

I control nothing, impress no one, a fallen leaf on
a stream, an unwilling passenger on another's current.
The humiliation I feel turns to something else—
surrender perhaps, or regret. Regret that I hadn't
known how to appreciate, regret that I hadn't thought a
few steps ahead. It's degrading to be a fool. Father
once told me: *Intelligence does not equal wisdom.* I
guess I'm the last to know.

People probably think my averted eyes are hiding
lies, but what I'm hiding has more to do with truth. In
truth, I'm a silly little fool. I can deny this reality and
try to wish it away, or I can accept it, and not waste
energy on wanting and wishing. I opt to accept it.

The slapper stares down at me. She arches an
eyebrow, proud that she has sprung her trap. All that
remains of me is a fool, and the world scorns a fool.

You silly little fool.

Father warned me not to ruin my life. Avoiding
corrosive people meant nothing to me. I let myself be
led by vain curiosities. Most cultures decide what girls
can and can't know, shielding them so they can go on
with their lives, unsullied. How I wish I had never
seen any of this. How I wish I could bury all this in
our ancient basement, where Father buried the original
first floor, and later, his painful memories.

I should have been better at saying *no*.

My fatal flaw was authorizing the world's worst people, Armand and Ava. I'm a nobody. It's clear that Ava doesn't like somebodies. Not many people ever see the real person behind Ava's mask . . . and live to tell about it. I can't say this emphatically enough: psychopaths make terrible traveling companions.

In a way, Ava *has* released me from my delusions. Unfortunately, I'll always live inside her words, they will shape me, conform me. But, death isn't enough to remove this humiliation. Suicide isn't my wish for death. It's the only way of avoiding decade after decade of truth. I'll become one huge pile of psycho. Make no mistake, insanity is an elegant solution for fallen women.

The crazy woman is one of nature's kindest solutions. I wonder if my friends will stop talking to me when I return from Moscow, now that I'm officially *crazy*? I'm almost thankful that I'll never see them again. I could live with that. Even the bitter cold of Moscow would be better than enduring their *soirées* with whispers and gapes. God must be the keeper of broken women or we are all doomed. This is the new me, my rock-bottom me. At least crazy is better than stupid.

I sit up, my bottom in the dirt, surrounded by the people who put me here. After my death, I intend to be the patron angel for anyone who has been pushed out of line, the last chosen, the person always ignored.

The metric we schoolgirls use to evaluate ourselves is so subjective—useless in the real world. The open market prefers commodities. What Ava's slap is trying to teach me is, I'm a commodity. This is the way things will be from now on—bullied. I'm empty and not okay with it. May Allah forgive me.

I fidget with the hem of my garment and brush away the dirt. I left home wearing my special Paris outfit, anxious for Armand to see it. This was the outfit that was supposed to change his mind, make him see me in a whole new way. I'm wearing shoes that poor Father had to work in blood for.

My father might have an appointment next week with one of these monsters who kidnapped his daughter. He would never know, and I could never point my finger and accuse them. I suppose it has always worked this way . . . fathers left to wonder.

I'd never thought of Father's work in those terms. These shoes, this outfit are whimsical fancies of a silly daughter. These pigs will remove my expensive clothes, steal my virginity, sell me, sell my clothes.

Father will probably see my clothes displayed on some discount rack in the marketplace, or see some peasant's wife wearing them. He'll vaguely think of me, not knowing why, not remembering that he bought those clothes, for me, that his daughter wore them, in his house. But Father will carry on while I disappear into the ether of consequence. Father once warned me: *Imagine a place without familiar landmarks. That's what being a teenager is like.* He was so right.

Sarah said, *A happy person will be happy wherever they are, an unhappy person will be unhappy wherever they are.* There may be some truth in this. God, I hope so. I should have been more content, more appreciative. I stink with ingratitude.

Stupidity reaches full blossom when you realize the person who smiled at you in private, intended to demean you in public. Ava wasn't my friend . . . and I'm not Giti's friend . . . not the kind of friend Giti needed.

It occurs to me; I don't hate politicians. I hate people who abuse power, no matter how small or fleeting that power is. Schoolgirls bully younger girls—abuse of power. Heartless women manipulate love-stricken men—abuse of power. Embittered mothers fill their sons with impossible obligations—abuse of power.

Men aren't always the abusers. Sometimes, they're victims. How many young men have ruined their lives trying to serve their motherland, live up to national duty? Sometimes men are so full of bad information that it takes a fair-minded woman to set them free.

Abuse of power has many faces. Ava's deceitful face will always loom over me. Maybe I have victims who see my face in their nightmares. After all, I wasn't good to Father. I wasn't kind to anyone, for that matter. There are as many women abusing power as men. It may take different forms, but the results are just as cruel. I would give anything to go home, tear up my note, and fix my mistakes—all my mistakes.

*   *   *

I managed to stand, albeit sad and wilted. Giti
edged her way over and hugged me, either from pity or
love.

Either was fine with me.

A wide-eyed optimist seldom comes to a good
end. I could never return to that gullible headspace of
naïve faith in others. Yet, I hoped Zoe and Sarah
would survive with their optimism intact. I wished my
hard-won wisdom on no one.

Giti led me a few steps away. She hid me among
the other girls, all lost, on the wrong side of love.
Whether betrayed, unwanted, or forgotten, we were a
sad lot. In my case, Armand was to blame. He changed
his mind and left me to predators of the night. There
was a right way to change his mind. He should have
been a man.

While I hid in Giti's arms, a shape emerged from
the darkness, small and determined. The closer it got,
the more Bosco it became. I was both heartened and
saddened. Poor Bosco. He too would be sold. Some
wealthy Russian would amuse his friends with a bike-
riding chimp. Bosco put his hands on my hips. All my
suppressed indignities exploded into tearful sobs. I had
no idea why he was here, but his feeble monkey hug
was my last connection to a world I would never see
again. I wouldn't get to say goodbye to anyone, except
this monkey.

Life can have a demented sense of humor.

A slaver pulled Giti aside and removed her makeshift tourniquet. He made a paste of pepper and water as a coagulant—a remedy common to soldiers. She moaned and twitched with pain. The slaver re-wrapped her thigh with clean gauze and bandages then leaned her against the back of his cargo truck. No one interfered with Bosco, not even Ava. The driver with the Pashtun cap broke out in a huge grin and approached Bosco, as if to shake his hand. The driver turned to the other men. "Look. It is Bosco, the champion rider!"

Bosco extended his hand, but snatched the pistol from the driver's waistband and gut-shot him. The driver fell to his knees, startled. He stared into Bosco's eyes until he fell, face down. For those few seconds, everyone was speechless. Then, more gunshots exploded from the dark perimeter and other slavers started dropping. All of a sudden, I'm in an action film. Sphincter-factor, very high. The rest of the slavers began stuffing girls into their lorries, Giti among them.

"Save me, Jamileh!" Giti cried out.

I turned in time to see the door slam, with Giti's face behind its bars.

"Quick Jamileh, unlock the door!"

A strong hand reached from the darkness and pulled me. My blood boiled up around my heart and compelled me to strike. I balled my fist and managed a wide swing to knock the slaver senseless. But his hand blocked my swing . . . and that's when I saw his face.

Uncle Solomon.

He continued firing an automatic rifle, single-handed, as he ushered me away from the caravan, away from lamplights, away from headlights. After his weapon ran out of bullets, Ava blocked our escape, pointing a large chrome pistol, aimed straight between Uncle Solomon's eyes.

"And so da tide has turned." Ava called to one of the few survivors from the other group. "Put her in da lorry. She knows her presumptuous little resistance iz over."

A sharp *pop* reverberated through the darkness, and Ava had a clean hole in her front teeth. She dropped her gun. Both hands quickly covered her mouth, but blood gushed through her fingers as she crumbled to the earth.

Bosco stood nearby with a smoking pistol.

Uncle Solomon rushed me through the darkness and Bosco wasn't far behind. Bullets *pinged* and *popped* all around us. Amidst it all, I stopped when I heard Giti call my name.

"Jamileh!" she called out. "Don't leave me!"

I started back, determined to knock the lock off her iron door. Uncle Solomon caught me and pulled me to the ground. At that point, I became fully aware of the bullets that *buzzed* past my ears like angry wasps.

"Jamileh!" Giti's voice called to me, raspy and ragged.

I crouched close to the earth and watched the lorry rumble away, northbound. Giti's face and voice shrunk smaller and smaller. I turned to Uncle Solomon. "Why don't you save her?" I turned again, helpless, and watched them take her away. She reached through the bars, calling my name . . . until she was gone.

Twenty

My Italian Valentinos were long gone, cast aside after Uncle Solomon threw me to the ground as we ducked bullets. Shoeless, I scrambled up the hillside, doing my best to keep up with Uncle Solomon and Bosco.

We were safe, for the moment. The slavers had fled in the opposite direction, due north. But even a full moon wasn't enough to save my toes from the stones on our escape path. The three of us struggled up the steep hillside—me faring the worst.

A bullet sparked against a rock, beside me.

Uncle Solomon spun around so fast he nearly lost his footing. "Another shooter? I should have known. Every crooked transaction has a sniper hidden on high ground." He pulled his pistol, but instead of shooting back, he returned it to his waistband and climbed faster toward the road above us.

Two shots rang out, almost simultaneous. That meant there were two shooters. Uncle Solomon continued moving me along as quickly as my sore feet permitted. He pointed to an excavated turnout on the road above. The *Monstrosity* gleamed in the moonlight just twenty yards away, the sweetest vision I'd seen all night. A bonus was strapped up top: a long bicycle.

It called to me.

In the far distance motorcycles growled to life. Uncle Solomon's head turned and searched the dark hill across from us. "They have motorcycles." His eyes lost their gleam. "That gives us less than a minute."

It seemed there were never enough Basij after sundown—when we needed them most. Where was God's army, the Mujahideen? And I was so close to home.

Just as we reached the *Monstrosity* the two motorcycles slid around a distant bend and thundered toward us. I heard gunshots, intent on our murder.

Bosco jumped through an open window, but Uncle Solomon pushed me in the back door and dashed toward the driver's side. Before entering, he pulled his pistol and fired, twice. The sound of motorcycles continued.

Blast his aim! He missed.

He jumped inside and turned the key. The engine cranked out a death rattle of *rur, rur, rur*. The starter moaned and quit. Uncle Solomon banged the steering wheel with both hands. "Not now!" He glared at Bosco. "Have you been listening to the radio?"

Bosco leaned away and did a curious thing with his lips, he tucked them in without confessing a thing.

The motorcycles came to a sliding stop, one on each side. At that very moment, the engine turned over and we left them in a flurry of dust.

From the backseat, I watched the back of Uncle Solomon's head—his lovely, noble head. He had come all this way to save me, and bought me a bike.

Bosco had the presence of mind to notice my tears of joy. He crawled into the back seat and wiped them away, comforting me with soft grunts and slow head nods. Nonetheless, I too suspected Bosco of draining the battery. Monkeys are thoughtless in that regard.

Bosco took my hand and covered it with both of his, top and bottom. This strange and wonderful monkey had turned the corner on manners. For someone who just shot Ava, he had a sensitive side.

"Did Armand send you?" I asked Uncle Solomon.

"No."

"You tracked me down and rescued me, all on your own?"

The hillside road was crooked, with many turns. The motorcycles were closing in.

"I am sorry to say this, but I had no idea you left the compound." Uncle Solomon winced as he negotiated his turns. "Imagine my surprise." He swerved to avoid a small boulder, fallen from the cliff above. "Imagine the coincidence." He swerved to avoid a wild donkey suddenly in our headlights. "Imagine how close you came to— Well, imagine my joy."

Armand was so thoughtless, and I was so unlucky. Whatever I hoped for never happened. I rocked back and forth, both hands pressed against my throbbing head. My feet were filthy with dust, mixed with Ava's blood.

I looked next to me, on the floorboard, and saw my London Fog carry-on. I hurried to zip it open and check the hidden pockets. Everything was dusty, but undamaged. Not a thing missing. "If you didn't know I was here, how did you find this?"

There wasn't a heartbeat between my question and Uncle Solomon's answer. "Bosco. He just loves the smell of diamonds."

Bosco shrugged like it was no big deal.

But it was a big deal! I remembered the day Uncle Solomon formally introduced us. Bosco had been sniffing at a diamond-encrusted Star of David. Suddenly, this monkey's idolatry shrank in importance. I had forgiven him for everything, including his running our battery down.

Uncle Solomon drove far too fast for Noshahr's dirt roads. Sometimes, when our tires lost their grip, we careened sideways. Not knowing what, or who we might hit, I gasped each time the *Monstrosity* slid into a curve. In the darkness, all that guided us was moonlight and the long rays of the car's headlamps. Half the time our headlights wagged left of center or right of center, useless for the road ahead. I wasn't sure who would kill me first, Uncle Solomon or the motorcycles behind us.

On winding roads, motorbikes had the advantage. Not that I remember, but I must have said something to that effect, because Uncle Solomon reassured me, "Only when we are moving." He hit the brakes and two successive *thuds* ended their threat.

Uncle Solomon gave Bosco a sly wink. "Motorcycles are great for chasing. Not so good for stopping."

*   *   *

We crested the hill overlooking Noshahr. Despite the darkness, I could make out all the familiar landmarks. I approximated where our compound should be. My room beckoned to me. I envisioned

Auntie Esther's tower on one side, and Uncle Solomon's on the other. A paradise framed in stone towers.

After we were halfway down the hill, safely away from the slavers, Uncle Solomon parked the car. He seemed anxious to show Bosco something. We all got out. Far below, I saw bicycles coming from all directions, headed north. Uncle Solomon put his arm around Bosco and pointed. The whole scene made Bosco very happy.

A mental fog parted and I was dimly aware of their unspoken manner of communication. "May the great prophet forgive me," I mumbled, afraid of the words about to come out of my mouth. "I think I'm starting to comprehend this monkey language."

Uncle Solomon sighed. "It is an uncanny thing, but he has a manner that conveys everything." He shrugged. "I cannot explain it either."

Bosco nodded and gazed past my eyes into my heart. He pointed toward Noshahr and bent his lips in an expressive slant.

Uncle Solomon interpreted: "We—Bosco and myself—have planned this night for months. Bosco unlocked the cages at the Monkey Bar before we left. Some monkeys will come from private homes, where they were kept as pets. Others have lived on the edge of civilization and will come out tonight for their great exodus. Some will ride bikes, some will drive cars, some will walk, but they are all headed for a new life in the forest, the Caspian Hyrcanian."

I gulped. "Drive cars?"

"They are very observant, and make no mistake, they have been watching." Uncle Solomon concluded with an emphatic nod.

"So, all those things down there, they're all monkeys?"

Uncle Solomon never answered, but Bosco raised his eyebrows and smiled.

I was stunned. I stared at Uncle Solomon in disbelief. "You trained all those monkeys?"

"Not a single one. Freedom is a force of nature with its own collective intelligence, a tide that enables every creature in its wake."

I put my hand over my mouth to hide one of those mouth-agape stares.

"In the car," Uncle Solomon commanded. "The moon dips low, and we're behind schedule."

"Where are we going?" I asked.

"To the zoo."

I didn't want to go to the zoo. I wanted to go home.

Bosco, in his excitement, took the front seat and pointed, directing Uncle Solomon toward the zoo.

I slammed the back door, bitter as vinegar. I was suddenly as anxious for home as I had been for Paris . . . and Uncle Solomon was talking crazy talk. How I longed for the heated soapstone that awaited my cold, bruised feet. "But, we'll be arrested."

Uncle Solomon's sly smile returned. "And who do you suppose oversees crime prevention?"

"The wolf who comes to us in wolf's clothing," I said. "Colonel Sohrabi."

"Exactly. He was called to Tehran, thanks to my well-timed complaints. Tonight, Sohrabi is in Tehran. He is a wolf on a fork. Tehran's Guardian Council turns the spit while the Ayatollah roasts him over the fiery coals of Islamic mandate. I triggered that investigation to clear the streets. As I said, we have planned this night to its last detail. Enough." Uncle Solomon smoothed the hair atop Bosco's head. "Destiny calls for this one."

As Uncle Solomon descended the hill, a lot of unsorted thoughts swirled through my head. How did I know to make my escape this night, of all nights? Had I sensed monkey liberation in the air? Unlikely. I had no powers of premonition. That was Sarah's domain. Me? Just a silly little fool. Maybe Iran would never formally recognize this as a day of national liberation, but in an odd, backwards, monkey way, the air bristled with joy, hope, and new beginnings.

After we entered town, we eventually came to the broad entrance of Noshahr Zoo. I knew where Bosco was headed, and I knew why. We parked beneath the weeping willow at the entrance. A reverent hush filled the car. All eyes were on Bosco.

"Do we have to go inside?" I emphasized *have to*.

Uncle Solomon shook his head. "Not you." He squeezed Bosco's shoulder. "But my friend has some ugly family business to conclude."

"No," I said. "Let's go home. Whether Sohrabi was called to Tehran or not, the Basij will certainly take Bosco into custody—and us."

"Jamileh, you know I take no joy in refusing you, but tonight is not about you."

Bosco swung his elbow over the seat and smiled at me. It was an at-peace smile.

Love hadn't come my way, tonight, but I was happy for Bosco . . . and Orange Peel.

Uncle Solomon reached over to put his pistol in the glove compartment, but Bosco grabbed his hand, pried the gun from his fingers, then tucked it under his armpit. Bosco lacked vestimentary options. Pockets.

"Are you sure?" Uncle Solomon asked.

Bosco nodded.

Uncle Solomon's lips fixed in a grim slant. He didn't seem at all pleased. "Well, do what you must."

Uncle Solomon motioned, inviting me to get out of the car. I did, reluctantly. Bosco, however, jumped out, anxious for what lay ahead, the pistol still under his armpit. Uncle Solomon unstrapped a tandem bicycle, jerry-rigged to the top of the *Monstrosity*. My heart fluttered with anticipation. Finally, I was about to ride a bicycle for the first time.

"It has a little basket," I said. "How cute."

"That is for Bosco's son. He will ride in the basket. Orange Peel will pedal from the rear, and Bosco will steer."

Bosco jumped behind the handlebars, leaning forward, like the champion that he was. Uncle Solomon asked for my assistance to give Bosco a push start. And through the gate Bosco went.

I didn't want to begrudge Bosco his bicycle, but I was saddened that a girl like me would never ride a bike. I had changed, but Iran was the same. "Just seems like a waste. How far do you think they'll get?"

"They will pedal until dawn. Then, at sunrise, they will hide their bicycle along the road and follow the tree line north, toward the Caspian Hyrcanian, forestland that stretches deep into Azerbaijan."

I smirked skeptically. Their plan sounded so preposterous. I said nothing, however. I couldn't explain in one-hundred years my new attitude, but I no longer had a heart for flippancy.

Still, my absence of enthusiasm made Uncle Solomon indignant. "Not exactly Africa, but with miles and miles of temperate forest, thousands of creeks and waterfalls, they should enjoy long comfortable lives. Their neighbors will be badgers, otters, geese, ducks. I expect Bosco will return occasionally to liberate other monkeys. Maybe he will start a Merry Band of Monkeys in the forest. This has been done before, in Sherwood Forest. More important, they will be together. That will be enough."

I was still skeptical, but this time I voiced the missing piece of the puzzle. "What about Shin Bone? Bosco has no teeth."

"Bosco will mortally wound Shin Bone with a bullet. His son will have last-blood rights, the only cure for his year of humiliation. Bosco's son has to learn bloodthirst to survive in the forest. He may as well begin tonight."

A gunshot echoed in the distance. I turned to Uncle Solomon, startled. "Bosco shot him."

"No. The first shot will tear the lock off. It is the second shot that will cripple Shin Bone. Then, Bosco's son will take his revenge. His son will wear Shin Bone's blood for the rest of the week. When it wears off, so will this dark chapter."

I looked down at the blood on my feet.

A sudden pall covered Uncle Solomon's face. "Oh no. How many shots did I fire from that gun? He may not have a second shot!"

A second shot rang out.

Uncle Solomon exhaled in great relief. He nodded as if he understood every sound. "In the coming months, I imagine some zoo keeper will discover another broken lock and a young female chimp missing. Bosco's son will have his new wife. Of course, their new life will have unexpected needs, but money is no obstacle. Bosco's nose can locate diamonds—cut or uncut. He knows how to trade. He's on a first-name basis with Mr. Oskou, our local pawnbroker."

I kept silent on that matter.

As someone who had recently escaped the icy grip of Russia, I could appreciate the sentiment: *They will be together*. No sweeter words on earth. Tonight, Bosco did more in the name of freedom than any Iranian politician. More than I did for Giti. Allah will punish me for that. And I will deserve it.

Uncle Solomon put his arm around me as we watched the three of them pedal out of the zoo's gate, each waved a final farewell—probably at Bosco's prompting.

Uncle Solomon waved back. "Commit this to memory. Pedaling from behind the handlebars is a father who never gave up. On the back seat, a mother who endured. In the basket, a son still crimson with his enemy's blood. They are living metaphors of Iran."

"Except, they're leaving."

"Yes. Except they are leaving."

"And they haven't changed one oppressive law."

"Yes. And they have not changed one oppressive law."

"And they will all be replaced with new monkeys before the end of the week."

"Yes. And they will all be replaced with new monkeys before the end of the week."

"And— "

Uncle Solomon pushed me toward the car, harder than necessary. I hadn't even finished my sentence!

"Get in the car," he said in a very brutish voice.

*   *   *

I took the front seat, desperate for a warm body and a little solace. I ignored my embarrassment. Uncle

Solomon drove us away from the zoo. He was upset, but I snuggled against him, anyway.

"I know you saw everything," I said, too ashamed to let him see my face.

"Yes," he said.

"And you saw them take Giti away."

"Yes."

"And you heard her call to me."

"To the last word."

"Do you despise me?"

"What you did was thoughtless, to family and friend. You must live with that."

His halting voice of reason censured me. It felt delicious and I never wanted it to stop.

"Facing that failure is your only hope. I am here to tell you that more failures are yet to come."

Lecture me about decency. I need it. Condemn me for selfishness. I'm guilty.

"Pray for Giti and yourself."

Punish me for ingratitude. I'll submit. My humiliation was inevitable. I knew it was only a matter of time.

"You are young," he said. "You have a lot of temporary in you. But, never confuse temporary with the permanent cosmic truths you are about to discover. That, Jamileh, is where wisdom lives."

I was about to burst with admiration for Uncle Solomon. He was right about everything. An angel had crossed my path. What a fool I'd been. Allah's best lived above our carriage house. Me? I had been a terrible friend, a terrible sister, and a terrible daughter. So sad to say, people like me make terrible wives. Giti would have been beating tambourines, walking three steps ahead of Uncle Solomon, proclaiming to everyone on the road: *A fine man approaches! Bow down. This miracle has been hiding amongst us.* Because, Giti was a better person than me.

How Christian I sounded, reverencing a Jew.

I would never be the same girl I used to be. Facing death, and being okay with it, changed me. Being thrown into a situation where I had nothing more to lose, and facing it, rewired my thinking, gave me a weird confidence. It also programmed me with a new shame, an ugly memory loop that I could never undo. I had escaped, but a fate worse than death awaited poor Giti. I would gladly trade places, if it would lessen this unbearable guilt.

"Uncle Solomon," I said, "a car is following us, and it's closing in fast."

The ideal reply should have been, *Oh, it's nothing, just a tractor on its way to the olive harvest.* But that's not what he said.

"Widely spread headlights. A government vehicle."

Uncle Solomon reached into the glove compartment, his fingers rummaged about. He smacked his forehead with the palm of his hand. "The monkey runs my battery down, then takes my only gun. I do not want to draw rash conclusions, but this certainly makes it hard to trust monkeys."

A thousand things could go wrong. And we were *so* close to home.

I leaned toward the passenger-side window and watched through the side mirror. Powerful headlights closed the distance between us. The cage of my chest nearly burst from holding my breath. That was no tractor, and it was already directly behind us, swerving, attempting to pull alongside. Maybe I was imagining things, but I thought I heard yelling.

Twenty-One

A long black Bentley zoomed parallel with Solomon's door. Shouts of celebration came from raucous boys as they passed, their car fishtailing the whole time. The government vehicle ripped the ground-layer of fog as it raced past us.

"It's Armand," Uncle Solomon said. His jaw tightened as he watched. "He will ruin that car."

In the distance, Armand veered off the dirt road into the soft sand and slowly tipped, lazily, gently, leaving the stately vehicle upside down.

I tugged at Uncle Solomon's arm. "We have to stop. Someone might be hurt."

"Armand will hurt, when the Ambassador sees his car, wheels up."

Uncle Solomon pulled over, just behind the Ambassador's car. Our headlights lit the scene, good as daylight. Armand slid through the driver's-side window. He helped two of his idiot friends as they climbed out laughing, unrepentant, staggering about like drunkards, singing unsanctioned melodies.

"The peacock's plumage is its undoing," sighed Uncle Solomon. "Stay in the car. And forgive me for what I am about to do."

He marched directly toward the group and socked Armand's friends into a state of unconsciousness. Armand backed away, waist deep in fog, holding his hands up defensively. Uncle Solomon kicked him in the balls, grabbed him by the collar, slapped him repeatedly until Armand's legs buckled and he dropped like a string puppet onto the sand.

Uncle Solomon walked back to our car and opened his door, but before getting in, he apologized. "I hope you did not see all that, but he nearly got you killed tonight."

I sat up straight and waggled my head. "He monkeyed with a girl and had to pay the organ grinder."

"Jamileh," Uncle Solomon enunciated with a whispery edge. "Vengeance does not become you."

I curled into myself, shamed.

My attempt at spiteful humor brought an icy glare from Uncle Solomon. "Too crudely put for someone of your importance. Let us not mention the subject again."

Coincidence.

I didn't *want* my outburst discussed again—nor anything else from this terrible night—so I nodded with enormous relief.

He looked over his shoulder at Armand, still flat on his back. "I doubt if he will remember anything, come morning."

"You're a dead man, Solomon Bijan!" yelled Armand.

Uncle Solomon climbed in, fastened his seatbelt, and stared far off toward the horizon. "He probably could have used a bit more slapping."

I warned Uncle Solomon against it with a grimace. "No more slapping. No more hitting."

He gave Armand a glowering squint of disapproval, and off we went.

An owl flew just above the fog, locked in the car's high beams, as if to guide us home. I leaned against Uncle Solomon's shoulder. His muscles were tense, his skin glowed like an oven.

"I have several small bags of diamonds hidden in the garage, thanks to Bosco." He gave me a nervous glance. "I may need them tonight."

I looked up, having no idea what that had to do with anything. I sensed a forthcoming explanation.

"If you don't see me tomorrow, be sure you let go of your self-pity and shame. Find meaning in what you have been through."

Uncle Solomon couldn't have said anything more hurtful. I didn't know how to find meaning. Giti's last words still rang in my ears. Where was the meaning in that? Armand had abandoned me without regard for my reputation. Being left alone wasn't the worst of it. Still wanting Armand, *that* was the worst of it. But make sense of all this? I couldn't.

I could go back to that farce of being a student at a private school. I could become that aqua engineer I had been so expensively trained for, but no amount of education could explain what I did tonight. Time would eventually take on my destruction as its main cause in life, and fools are defenseless against such onslaughts.

"Life reveals the fool in all of us, sooner or later," Uncle Solomon said. "With enough of these life lessons, maybe mankind will create a safe corner somewhere, a decent place for children. Maybe there will be a child in my future. After all, the apocalypse didn't come, the revolution didn't kill us, no cybergeddon, and I see no Messiah on the horizon. Yet, here we are. Still surviving."

Something was wrong. His words seemed so unfitted to our successful return home. I wanted to interrupt him. I had a whole riff of long overdue apologies.

His hand gripped my forearm. "I know what you are thinking. Do not be so hard on yourself. If we all confessed our sins, we would laugh at our unoriginality."

The sight of our compound caused my chest to rise and fall with deep breaths of relief. The closer we came, the more my fears dissipated.

"Uncle Solomon?"

"Yes, little Jamileh."

"Don't you think it's time to drop the 'little'?"

"You are exactly right, Jamileh."

I sat on my knees and watched his face. Not so much as a smirk. What a refreshing surprise. I sat back against the passenger door, absorbing the new moniker. It was official, I was a woman with a capital *W*.

Solomon winked at me.

Both of us sighed at the same time.

Clearly, his winks had magical powers, because I swear, if he asked me to jump out of the car—at full speed—and then winked, I would have jumped, head first. For the first time in years, I felt his playfulness, like an old friend had showed up, after a long absence.

He smiled and shook his head.

I wondered if I should smile. Did smile. Then I wondered why, why he smiled and why I smiled back. I didn't know what we were doing—at all. "Solomon? I just want to ask a simple question. And don't just say something polite." I took a deep breath. "Do you think Allah will ever forgive me?"

"Because of what you did to Giti?"

Her memory brought a lump to my throat. All I could do was stare into the dark floorboard. "To everyone . . . but, especially Giti."

"I stopped you from going to her. He will take that into consideration."

"But for the part I played, which was more than you might think, will Allah ever forgive me?"

"I know the question well," he said. "I have been asking it for years. What more could I have done to save my sisters . . . which was more than you might think."

I hurt for him. Had he blamed himself all these years? We were getting closer to home, and I had so much more I wanted to say, but our high beams were already on the garage door.

Solomon braked gently, then stepped out and pushed the garage's sliding door open. He got back inside, drove into the carriage house and parked, straight and neat.

He stared at the steering wheel, deep in thought. Finally, he turned to me with a long face. "That kid has a head full of bad wiring. If I stayed, he could not live with my knowing so. Armand is the son of an ambassador, and now, a member of the Basij. He will bring them before the sun reaches high noon and blame me for wrecking his father's car." He gripped my head at both temples. "Tell them I said rude things about Iran and stole your bike. Tell them I went north, on your bicycle, to join the Olympic team in Azerbaijan."

There it was, the dreaded announcement I suspected earlier. I had no bicycle. Solomon was sacrificing himself, for the safety of our family. He would become the second victim of my escapade, and without him, I would be the third.

Solomon got out, and lit an oil lamp that hung on the carriage-house wall.

I climbed out and stood beside him, not speaking at first, but willed him to stay with all my psychic forces.

His dark eyes shimmered beneath the oil lamp. As we stood there, enveloped in the lamp's small globe of light, the intimacy within its flicker gave an exaggerated import to our silhouettes.

Shakespearean.

Mere words could not live up to such a stage.

"I love you, Solomon."

He didn't return my smile, but by his expression, I could tell he was pleased.

"I am not really going to Azerbaijan," he confessed. "I am headed south, for Israel. Maybe it is too much to expect your family to make the journey to Jaffa, but that is where I must go. If ever you do visit, I will teach you how to ride a bicycle."

I leaned closer. "I didn't mean like a brother." As I mouthed these words we looked at each other with an emotion that neither of us concealed. I raised my chin, lips pursed, awaiting his kiss.

Solomon leaned back, about the same distance I had leaned in. "I was afraid you would say that."

My eyes burned at the offense. "Why?"

"Because I cannot imagine where that goes, and neither can you."

I came close to objecting. Girls my age, after all, were marrying. I buttoned my lip, instead. I tried for a smile, but missed. He knew why I left home, tonight. I had no credibility, no right to speak of love. None.

Yet, he reassured me, gripping both my shoulders. "The years will instruct us. Time will tell." He pulled open a drawer beneath the lamp and pulled out three small bags. He put one in his backpack and placed two in my hands, one in each palm. "Give these to your father."

I gripped the bags and felt small stones grind against themselves. Bosco diamonds.

"Today your father enjoys a comfortable life in Iran, but who can say what tomorrow will bring."

The bags were small, but weighty. I slipped them into the pockets of my dusty jilbab coat.

"A day may come," he said with a heavy sigh, "when this is all you can take. This fortune travels light, easy to conceal. If the good doctor ever needs a place to stay, a safe home for his daughters, that day would be the best day of my life. What's mine, is

his—forever." When his smile disappeared, a fresh
spirit stoked a dream-like flame behind his eyes until
they shimmered like stars bright enough to wish on.
He patted his backpack where his diamonds made a
bulge. "And a fine home I will have."

I drew a wounded breath and wiped away a tear.
Any words that came from my mouth would be cheap.
I'd already tarnished that word, *love*, but that was
when I was fourteen. This time, it came from someone
almost fifteen. "You'll see." That's as close as my
words dared. I just couldn't bring myself to utter that
word again.

He led me to the courtyard, but returned to the
garage while I waited. He came out with his European
racing bike, a backpack full of I-don't-know-what,
along with my London Fog carry-on. I had completely
forgotten about my carry-on. Maybe my values had
improved. He rolled it in front of me and made a
sweeping gesture of deliverance.

He placed four fingers beneath my chin, while his
thumb rubbed my chin's edge. He gave me a lazy
smile.

I held my breath.

His smile oozed patience. I was confused. That
was more than a brother's smile.

"Shut the gate when I leave." Without another
word, he walked his bike toward the gate. He threw
me a salute, imitating a sailor casting off. It was
quaint. It gave our farewell a comical Hollywood flair.
He was funny again, like when we were kids.

"Girls wear shorts in Tel Aviv," I bellowed. ". . . or, so I've heard." I put my hand over my mouth. What a silly thing to say, but he needed to be warned.

He raised a cautionary hand, urging me not to follow.

I didn't. I watched him leave through our gate, our huge gate with large cedar planks and strong iron hinges.

Somewhere between the blue of night and the gold of day, in darkness before dawn, he left me. The distant whir of bicycle gears meant he was on his way—due south. Fanning off a blush of passion, I realized how impossible our odds were. My heart resisted, but I did the numbers. There's a heartless practical side to love.

Damn practicality!

If I had one iota of courage I would chase behind that man, running, crying like a fool the whole way. Certainly after five miles, he would realize how serious I was.

But Solomon was pedaling toward Israel, and I wasn't chasing him.

What a silly little fool I was. It doesn't matter how many trips a man makes to Mecca, how many infidels he has rebuffed. How a man treats others says it all. Nothing made Solomon's words sparkle brighter than the way he treated my father. He was a man we could trust. Women sense that sort of thing. They don't always know where it comes from, but they know when it's there and when it's not.

Solomon had seen me at my worst. If he had asked me to leave with him, I would have, even if it meant going to that godawful Jaffa. It was all such bad timing. I'm not ready for Jaffa. I lacked the demeanor that a grown man needs. I may as well hold up a sign that says: WARNING! NEEDS THOUSANDS OF HOURS OF WORK.

I hoped Solomon would remember my better days. May he frame me in those gilded memories, when I was sweet and innocent. Sometimes you have to travel back in time, skirting the worst parts, in order to love someone.

I put my hand on the latch of Father's front door.

I suppose a daughter could know a thing to death, and still be completely ignorant of it. I had underestimated Father. A girl could know her father yet see nothing but genetics and authority. Yet, there was a time, when I faced darkness and knew his hand was not too far away. My fingers could see in the dark to find his.

I have a great father—unappreciated, but great.

Maybe every bad daughter imagines herself a victim, forced into rebellion, sincerely believing she'd been mistreated. Repulsion, propulsion, momentum. Necessary for every generation who wants to be launched into their own universe. It pained me to think that I was predictable, ordinary, a cliché.

But I was.

I skulked all the way up our spiral staircase. Our home was always quiet at this time of night. Safe. Instead of going straight to my room, I veered left, and went outside to the terrace. As I hoped, Solomon's distant figure ascended a distant hill. He was framed in the moon's silver orb. Then, descending behind the hill, he was forever gone.

Most young men are such bores. They haven't lived long enough to learn they are not the wonders their mothers imagine. Solomon wasn't boring. Quiet, but never a bore.

I went to my room. Waiting at the foot of my bed was a heated soapstone, Sarah's proof of love. How I loved Sarah, Zoe, Father . . . my home. I closed my eyes and swooned with gratitude. Whoever you are, you don't know who you are. Why had I been so anxious to summarize my life when I was so far from the final chapter?

A cold chill gripped my spine. The front gate was still unlocked. Afghan slavers were out there, filled with hate and revenge. I swirled down our spiral staircase to barricade against the dark tendrils of human traffickers. With every step my anxieties got louder, multiplied.

I rushed to the front gate, but lingered, confused. I touched my chin, where Solomon's thumb once slid over my skin. It awakened feelings much deeper than the brief experience. Retracing his touch painted a beautiful memory that would stay with me, forever. I slid my fingers lightly over my chin, again and again. I closed my eyes and moaned, downhearted.

I looked at the latch and nearly swung the gate open, instead of locking it, still wondering if I could catch Solomon.

I wasn't worth it.

I had nothing to contribute to that good man's life. I put both hands on the large iron latch. But instead of swinging it open, I pushed hard to lock it, to safeguard myself, my family, my honor . . . or what was left of it. *Click, clang, grind, zing, clap, schlik.*

No choice better than this. No fork in the road that had any appeal. No silly dream was worth the risk.

I tiptoed inside the house, closing the door quietly behind me. I started to turn toward my room, but stopped. Instead, I doubled-back to check its locks and latches. *Click, clang, grind, zing, clap, schlik.*

Safe.

At last.

Twenty-Two

Two weeks of thoughtless self-indulgence. Now, my free hours are spent at Noshahr's docks, passing out flyers to Russian sailors. *I'll pay cash (one-million-seven-hundred-thousand French francs—enough for a small apartment in Paris) for one Iranian girl who goes by the name of Giti Khan.*

I visit synagogues: *Do you know a Solomon Bijan? He now resides in Jaffa.* I keep a letter I penned, hoping some Jew will deliver my sentiments on their next journey to Israel. It's filled with the tender thoughts I was too confused to speak when Solomon left me.

On my best days Giti's voice is barely audible. On my worst days, I'm blinded by tears of regret. Giti fell on the wrong side of opportunity, maybe with an unintended shove from me.

I often stand at the shoreline where Mother took Giti and me for picnics. I console myself with Edgar Dark-Gruesome-Emo-Laden Poe as the sun sets:

> *I stand amid the roar*
> *Of a surf-tormented shore,*
> *And I hold within my hand*
> *Grains of the golden sand—*
> *How few! yet how they creep*
> *Through my fingers to the deep,*
> *While I weep—while I weep!*
> *O God! can I not grasp*
> *Them with a tighter clasp?*
> *O God! can I not save*
> *One from the pitiless wave?*

I thought I knew what a wall was. Now, when anyone asks, I explain that in my Jamilehverse, I once hindered others with such high expectations that I lived behind an inevitable wall of disappointment.

That wasn't fair. For most people, life doesn't get any better. Most of us are stuck in the same town, stuck in the same routine, stuck in a life that provides just enough oxygen to breathe.

I shame know-it-alls who belittle the garments of orphan girls. Like an orphan's life isn't difficult enough?

Adolescence corrodes the innocent sheen of childhood. We know-it-alls spend the rest of our lives repairing the damage we've done to others. Life has a way of forcing us to come to terms with all that. Everything is really a battle against ourselves. If we're lucky, an angel shows up and lends a helping hand. For me, my angel was Solomon.

Dear, dear Solomon.

Somewhere along the way, I sensed I needed something from a fellow human, long before I had a word for it. Apparently, I was surrounded by angels who were with me the whole time. How unfortunate that I didn't recognize my special angel until he was gone.

Iran may not be particularly enlightened, peaceful or fun. We no longer have a Monkey Bar, nevertheless, we have intelligence good enough to cultivate; we can plant anything in that. Here we are, alive and attempting to fill our daily lives with what little joys we can.

How hard my dear father slogs in our service. Never getting, never expecting a *thank you*. I close my eyes, knowing quite well, he'll die within these four walls, without proper accolades.

Dear, dear Father.

I wake up each day in his beautiful home, where life is orderly, without so much as a wrinkle; where everything important is in the right place. It's a long road home for those of us who live selfishly, but there may be no road home for Giti . . . because she trusted me.

Dear, dear Giti.

Will I ever see beyond me? Am I capable? If you can do nothing else, do whatever is in your power to make people in your life feel completely unashamed of who they are. I fear what every right-thinking person fears, that my selfish heart will go back to what it wants. That's my biggest fear—that I might try it all again.

When I see how my whims affect my family, my friends, the temptations of France seem paltry and few. I came back thinner, paler, weaker, more cynical. Maybe I'm not the free spirit I pretended to be.

Twenty-foot walls contain me quite well. True, I still ache for freedom, but not out there. From what I've seen, people are climbing over each other to find their own secret garden, their own safe place. I can't blame them. We all need a twenty-foot wall.

I've got mine.

# # #

Michael Benzehabe

Author; Guest Speaker; Columnist: and All-Around-Really-Nice-Guy

Michael Benzehabe has written award-winning fiction, such as *Unassimilated,* and has a soon-to-be-released novel in the works, *Zonked Out.*

If you book guest speakers and want Mr. Benzehabe at your book club, reading group, or social-cause group, stay current with his speaking itinerary. If he's nearby, he may be available to stop in and inspire members.

S t a y I n T o u c h:

Book Stores: Wholesale ordering for *Persianality* www.amazon.com/dp/109550844X. **Media Interviews:** Television; Radio; and Journalists (Michael Rankin: mike_rankin@rocketmail.com). **Speaking Engagements:** Subjects tailored to your organization's needs (Michael Benzehabe: benzehabe@gmail.com). **Syndicated Column:** (Max Reagan: syndication@benzehabe.com). **Social Network:** www.linkedin.com/in/michael-ben-zehabe-31aa0942; facebook.com/michael.benzehabe; https://youtu.be/M4-MYNj9YU0. **Web Page:** www.amazon.com/author/benzehabe

Suggested Questions for Book Clubs

Chapters One through Two
1. Does Jamileh hate Iran?
2. What does Jamileh want?
3. Who can Jamileh rely on?
4. Any hints of hyperbole?
5. Which family member is missing?

Chapters Three through Four
1. Describe Jamileh.
2. Describe Jamileh's home.
3. What did you discover about Jamileh you didn't see in previous chapters?
4. What is it about restraint that scares Jamileh?
5. Why is Zoe living in the Delkash home?

Chapters Five through Six
1. What rivalry exists between Jamileh and her sisters?
2. What freedoms does Dr. Delkash grant Zoe?
3. What job does Jamileh give Zoe?
4. Does Jamileh exhibit prejudices?
5. Who is Colonel Sohrabi, and what has he got to do with Jamileh?

Chapters Seven through Eight
1. How old is Ava?
2. Describe the Monkey Bar.
3. Why is Bosco forced to race at the Monkey Bar?
4. How did Ava and Jamileh meet?
5. Giti relays what news about Armand?

Chapters Nine through Ten
1. Who, or what, is interfering with Zoe's primary goal?
2. Who unlatches the doors every night?
3. What is cliethrophobia?
4. Are Muslims allowed to drink alcohol on special occasions?
5. How does Jamileh feel about her father remarrying?

Chapters Eleven through Twelve
1. Describe Auntie Esther.
2. Is Auntie Esther prejudiced?
3. What invitation was delivered to the Delkash compound?
4. Does Sarah and Zoe know they were invited to the Monkey Bar?
5. Jamileh imagines what will happen in Paris?

Chapters Thirteen through Fourteen
1. What happens to Giti at the Monkey Bar?
2. Why does Ava remind Jamileh of her mother?
3. What is Ava's escape plan?
4. How is Jamileh's escape plan progressing?
5. Does Jamileh's problem with authority affect her view of men?

Chapters Fifteen through Sixteen
1. What character flaw surfaces in Jamileh?
2. What new things has Jamileh discovered about Uncle Solomon?
3. Is it possible Jamileh is overly dramatic?

4. How is Jamileh's relationship with Armand evolving?
5. Why does Armand keep asking about Sarah?

Chapters Seventeen through Eighteen
1. Does Giti have an escape plan?
2. How does Giti change to accommodate Jamileh?
3. Why does Jamileh proclaim God bless America?
4. Does Jamileh tell the truth in her note?
5. What happens to Jamileh's inheritance?

Chapters Nineteen through Twenty
1. Jamileh has struck other characters. Why the sudden concern about what a slap is?
2. Any passages that relate to bullying?
3. Who are Jamileh's friends and who are her enemies?
4. Has Jamileh stolen Giti's freedom?
5. By contrast, who got their freedom and who didn't?

Chapters Twenty-One through Twenty-Two
1. Who is more self-deluded, Jamileh or Armand?
2. Why did Jamileh stop using "Uncle" when addressing Solomon?
3. Why does Solomon have to leave Iran?
4. Why doesn't Jamileh leave with Solomon?
5. What new revelation has Jamileh discovered?

Bonus Questions

1. What's the difference between thesis, antithesis, and synthesis?
2. Has Jamileh changed since chapter one?
3. In the eyes of Jamileh, have new character strengths surfaced in others?
4. Is Jamileh dangerous to the people around her?
5. Who has the most Persianality?
6. Did Jamileh's story change any opinions you started with?
7. Any favorite lines worth quoting?
8. Cover photo depicts a scene from what chapter? (pg 56)